PENGUIN BOOKS
HER STORY SO FAR

Monica Das has been a part of the faculty of Delhi University for over thirty years. Her work on gender studies has been recognized by several universities abroad and she has presented papers on gender issues at various international conferences. She writes articles on India's culture and heritage for several popular journals.

She is currently Reader, Economics, at Gargi College, New Delhi.

D1523858

Her Story So Far

Tales of
the Girl Child
in India

EDITED BY
MONICA DAS

PENGUIN BOOKS

PENGUIN BOOKS
Published by the Penguin Group
Penguin Books India Pvt Ltd, 11 Community Centre, Panchsheel Park, New
Delhi 110 017, India
Penguin Group (USA) Inc., 375 Hudson Street, New York, New York 10014,
USA
Penguin Group (Canada), 10 Alcorn Avenue, Toronto, Ontario, Canada M4V
3B2 (a division of Pearson Penguin Canada Inc.)
Penguin Books Ltd, 80 Strand, London WC2R 0RL, England
Penguin, Ireland, 25 St Stephen's Green, Dublin 2, Ireland (a division of Penguin
Books Ltd)
Penguin Group (Australia), 250 Camberwell Road, Camberwell, Victoria 3124,
Australia (a division of Pearson Australia Group Pty Ltd)
Penguin Group (NZ), cnr Airborne and Rosedale Road, Albany, Auckland
1310, New Zealand (a division of Pearson New Zealand Ltd)
Penguin Group (South Africa) (Pty) Ltd, 24 Sturdee Avenue, Rosebank,
Johannesburg 2196, South Africa

Penguin Books Ltd, Registered Offices: 80 Strand, London WC2R 0RL, England

First published by Penguin Books India 2003

This anthology copyright © Penguin Books India 2003
Introduction copyright © Monica Das 2003
The copyright for individual pieces vests with the contributors.
Page 193 is an extension of the copyright page.

Typeset in Sabon by R. Ajith Kumar, New Delhi

Printed at Baba Barkhanath Printers, New Delhi

'. . . only the story . . . can continue beyond . . . It is the story . . . that saves our progeny from blundering like blind beggars into the spikes of the cactus fence. The story is our escort; without it, we are blind.

Does the blind man own his escort? No, neither do we the story; rather it is the story that owns us and directs us.'

—*Anthills of the Savannah*
Chinua Achebe

Contents

Acknowledgements

My deepest thanks to Dr S.Y. Quraishi for his valuable suggestions, critical assessment and words of encouragement; Dr Pratibha Ray for helping me out with the translation of 'Rebati' and for being a well-wisher; Dr Geeta Dharmarajan and Shoma Chowdhury for their help and cooperation; Mahasweta Baxipatra for meticulously screening the Introduction; Dr Minoti Chatterjee and Dr Kamlesh Malhotra for always being there to offer correct advice when I needed it; Professor J. Misra of the University of Texas, Austin, and my friends Dr Rajalakshmi Rath and Mrs Subhalakshmi Misra for keeping my spirits buoyant; Mr V.N. Sharma for untiringly typing out the manuscript for me; and my husband, Udayabhanu, and my two sons, Kaustubh and Arunabh, for their invaluable moral support.

Introduction

It is well established that girls in many countries and continents experience the 'apartheid' of gender from the time they are born. Their fundamental rights to nutrition, health care, education, equality in access to opportunities and, often, survival are restricted or even denied, and they are considered easy prey to physical and emotional exploitation.

The situation, so far as the 171.50 million girls in the age group of 0-14 years in India are concerned, is considerably disturbing. The sex ratio which has always been unfavourable to girls has been deteriorating since Independence. Since 1991, the population of female children has been less than that of male children at all ages below fourteen. In fact, the 2001 Census clearly shows a decline in the number of females per thousand males in the most literate and prosperous states, especially in the 0-5 age group. Girls are exposed to a greater risk of death between the first and fifth year of their lives, the risk being 45 per cent higher where girls are concerned. Only 54.16 per cent of the female population above seven is literate as opposed to 75.85 per cent among males in the same age group. Broadly speaking, only 50 per cent of the girls participate in the education process and the stagnation and dropout rate is also alarmingly high compared to that of boys. Out of 11.28 million child workers, 5.10 million are female and nearly 50 per cent of them work as domestic help in urban areas and in hazardous industries. Around 30 per cent of the sex workers in India are below eighteen, and 40 per cent of them were inducted into the trade before they turned fourteen. As much as 47 per cent of the girl child population of India is malnourished. And, most startling of all, children alone account for 19 per cent of the total number of rape victims in this country. Speaking of crime against girls, in the year 2000 alone, selling of girls for prostitution went up by 15.3 per cent, female foeticide by 49.2 per cent and female infanticide by 19.5 per cent. Everyday, the newspapers abound with reports of paedophiles, traffickers, dowry-demanders and abusive parents.

Practices of gender inequality greatly influence the socialization process of women in India. Most households, even today, prefer male children to female, because 'they will carry on the family name'. Thus the ever-increasing numbers of female infanticide and female foeticide every year. The IMR (Infant Mortality Rate) at the national level is relatively higher for females than males. The rural areas record an IMR of 75, which is almost double that in the urban areas, where it is 44. Girls are consistently short-changed when it comes to their share of the basic resources of food, education and health care, because a lower value is placed on their survival and well-being. A girl infant is often breast-fed for a shorter period and is taken less often to a health care centre than a male infant. In fact, one out of three girl children in India does not live to see her fifteenth birthday. Girls also have a lower rate of immunization and receive less physical nurturing than their brothers. All this is justified with facile excuses such as 'girls need less food than boys because boys work harder' or 'girls need not be educated because they will get married soon and leave their homes'.

Data courtesy: Census of India 2001; National Family Health Survey (1998–99); Annual Report of the Department of Women and Child Development (2002–2003), Ministry of Human Resource Development, Government of India.

Introduction

Creative practice invariably imitates life, and literature is almost always a true reflection of the society that it is a product of. The ensemble of short stories brought together in this collection brings before the reader the predicament in which the majority of girls in India find themselves. Written by eminent writers from different regions of India, these stories provide unique perspectives on the way Indian society regards its women. Each story, a masterpiece in its own right, is a result of deep insight, acute sensitivity and the finest craftsmanship.

We are made privy to the life of a young girl called Shanichari who belongs to a tribal community and is sucked into a vicious cycle of exploitation by poverty and unfortunate circumstances. A literary rendering of the institutionalized discrimination against women workers, particularly those belonging to the lower strata of society, this powerfully written story by Mahasweta Devi directly indicts society as a whole for the cruelty meted out to the young girl. Similarly, Baburao Bagul's 'Death Comes Cheap' is a story about the life of women who live on the streets of a bustling city. The story is a brutal reminder that poverty is yet another socio-economic factor that contributes to the exploitation of women. Incidentally, women in India account for about 70 per cent of the people living below the poverty line. Kamala Das's 'A Doll for Rukmani' deals with the trafficking of girls and the total disregard for their safety from diseases and unwanted pregnancies, while Phakirmohan Senapathy's 'Rebati' dwells on the difficulties a young girl has to face in her quest for education. Although written more than a century ago, the story has a contemporary appeal, for the scenario remains distressingly similar to this day.

Gender constructs pervade every stage of a girl's life. In Mrinal Pandey's 'Girls', a little girl, unable to comprehend why she cannot be accepted for who she is, is left wondering, 'Do mother birds too think their girl birds are inferior?' Pratibha

Ray's 'Mushi' portrays the predicament of a young girl who is used and exploited for the sole purpose of bearing a legal heir. In 'Mushi' a further fact of emphasis and dramatization lies in the woman's inherently temporary membership in her natal group. Her realization that her existence is completely functional as far as her husband and her brother are concerned is tragic. Ultimately, when her son, who is the only meaningful entity in her otherwise pointless existence, is torn away from her, it brings about her demise.

Often, in our society, excessive value is attached to traditional roles and responsibilities. A woman's choices are made for her because it is assumed (and she is conditioned into believing) that she can't make her own. She is taught from a very young age the appropriateness and inappropriateness of her behaviour—she should not talk loudly, she should sit with her legs crossed or her knees together, she should spend less time studying and more time doing household work, she should not question the decisions taken by her father or her brother about how she should live her life . . . the list goes on. In 'Izzat', by Ashapurna Devi, an educated woman is forced to accept her husband's decision to refuse a young, helpless girl shelter for a night. The story exposes the silent complicity of women that helps reinforce oppressive patriarchy. More often than not, girls are conditioned into accepting and internalizing the norms that discriminate against her. Thus, in 'Kanjak', superstitions and notions of purity and virginity have been so strongly instilled in her mind that Daropati succumbs to shock when she realizes that her niece has lost her virginity before her marriage. In 'I See the Yamuna on the Horizon' by Indira Goswami, a girl who belongs to a well-to-do family learns from an uneducated girl what it means to be a woman and that it is not wrong to feel passion for a man. Interestingly, she wishes that her child is born a girl who can learn to think and act for herself and develop her own sense of right and wrong. In 'The Swing', by J. Bhagyalakshmi, Pankajakshi, an elderly woman, gathers enough courage to sit on the swing and enjoy herself without the fear of being ridiculed or reprimanded only after she watches her granddaughter swinging high in the air without the least bit of fear.

A question frequently asked regarding women has been, why women seem to accept and reinforce oppression towards themselves and other women around them. In 'A Memory Called Ammacchi' by Vaidehi, Seetatte is instrumental in perpetuating the cruelties that an outsider inflicts on her own daughter, Ammacchi. Fortunately, Ammacchi is a rebel at heart and gets the better of her tormentor. Ambai's 'My Mother, Her Crime' provides evidence that the passage from childhood to womanhood is tremendously difficult for a large segment of the female population. In Ambai's story, the little girl expects her mother to be her support through a difficult time in her life when she cannot comprehend the changes taking place in her body. But her mother, preoccupied with other things and completely insensitive to her daughter's needs at that moment, betrays her.

A very different subject is explored in Ismat Chughtai's brilliantly conceived story 'The Quilt'. It portrays a lesbian relationship between the beautiful wife of a wealthy landlord and her maid as seen through the eyes of a child. The story gives us remarkable insight into a child's innocent mind that witnesses everything but concludes little from the experience and makes no judgements.

What is remarkable is that though these stories originate from different linguistic, cultural and social backgrounds, all of them are concerned with a common objective—to portray the truth about the status of the girl child in India and, perhaps, to instill awareness and a sense of responsibility in those who read them. The realization must dawn that despite the stray instances of positive change in the socio-economic indicators, a lot more needs to be done in terms of developing and implementing gender sensitization; that political will and civil society networks must be strengthened and mobilized to combat abuse against the girl child.

Most significantly, these stories celebrate the spirit of the girl child and her determination to keep hope alive, even as they describe the dismal prospects that surround her.

—Monica Das

Mahasweta Devi

Shanichari

When Shanichari was a girl of twelve, she went to the haat in Tohri. And why not? After all, they enjoyed the train ride to Tohri, sitting on the floor of the compartment, chugging along, having a good time picking the lice from each other's hair. Shanichari had gone with her grandmother, her eng-ajji. Eng-ajji knew all sorts of age-old tales and stories. She didn't often find a willing audience. The old woman could hardly hear, but she loved telling stories.

After they got on the train, Shanichari settled her grandmother with her back against a wall. She said, 'Thakuma, tell us that story about the foolish son-in-law. It'll pass the time.'

'That one? All right.'

'Go on, start.'

'The foolish son-in-law was on his way to his in-laws'. He walked and walked. Suddenly—who's following him? Must be another man going the same way. Didn't realize it was his shadow. So the stupid man offered the shadow a pithey and said, "Here, eat this."'

Shanichari collapsed with laughter at this point. What a fool! Offering food to his own shadow! But eng-ajji never managed to finish a story. She would fall asleep half-way.

'Oh, Thakuma, sleeping again?'

'Then the sindoorwalla said, "I'll marry the girl. I've given her sindoor. And so she's mine."'

'Which story is that?'

'Why? Don't you know the one about the carpenter who carved her out of wood and became her father? The weaver who gave her clothes and became her brother? The goldsmiths who gifted her jewellery and became her uncles? Didn't the sindoorwalla bring her to life by giving her sindoor?'

'You mean the story of the four friends?'

'How would you know it? Nice story, isn't it? When we were young, the boys would all go to the jonkha-erpay[1] and we girls would go to the pel-erpay.[2] Stay up all night listening to stories. Singing songs. Those were the days.'

The old woman had fallen asleep again. Shanichari was leaning against the window. How wonderful it was, this freedom! Today she didn't have to graze the goats, pick firewood or cook the rice. She could just run free. Outside the window, trees-huts-fields-hills streamed past her and Shanichari felt as if she was rushing ahead.

'Hey, careful! Don't stick your head out of the window.'

Hiralal called out to her. Hiralal wandered from train to train with a harmonium around his neck, singing songs. No one knew how old he was. Even women who were mothers several times over could remember him unchanged. Hiralal's address—the shade of a tree, the side of a road. He had a wizened look, a shabby shirt and pants, a pair of slippers.

Startled, Shanichari drew back.

'You'll get coal dust in your eyes.'

Shanichari didn't reply.

'Come, sit here. Aren't you Moti Linda's daughter?'

---

[1] jonkha-erpay: Traditional tribal youth commune for boys.
[2] pel-erpay: Traditional tribal youth commune for girls.

'Yes.'

'I know. From Chotti tehsil, aren't you?'

'Yes.'

'I keep track of everyone. Mongru who got jailed was from your village, no? Is he free now?'

'Oh yes, ages back.'

'Didn't the panchayat meet? On his return from jail, didn't he feast you all? Is it all over?'

Shanichari shook her head. 'Mongru went off to Kolkatta. Said he'd earn some money, come home and then treat us.'

'Kolkatta?'

'Yes, yes. Many of them have left.'

'Where to?'

'To the brick kilns.'

A plump female wrapped in a yellow sari had been dozing all this while. She woke up now. Yawning, she said, 'Good for them. Why starve to death in the village?'

'Gohuman Bibi, is it you?'

'Who the hell are you?'

'Look carefully, you've seen me before.'

'Oh! Hiralal!'

'Where are you off to?'

'Tohri haat.'

'Fishing again?'

'Enough of your jokes.'

'I'm not joking. You must have cast your net already. Nandi must have been sent ahead to find out everything. When you arrive she'll tell you the number of girls per village. You'll go back to Kolkatta and get the requisite amount of money from the malik. Come back and treat the villagers to a slap-up meal of meat and rice, throw in liquor too. Tell the girls, why bother starving to death here? Come with me. Work in the brick kilns. Come to Kolkatta. You'll make money, get new saris.'

'So? Don't I find them work in the brick kilns?'

'You're Gohuman all right![3] A cobra spits venom, like you. You sell off the girls. Twenty rupees per girl. Supply a thousand girls and make twenty thousand.'

'What about cuts? Me, a cobra? It's the malik who's the snake. His musclemen take money from me.'

'What you are doing is a terrible sin, don't you know that?'

Gohuman shook her head. She said, 'What do you mean, sin? What kind of sin? What makes you so holier-than-thou?' She began counting on her fingers and said, 'Wait a minute. Let me explain. The malik runs a brick kiln. He needs rejas. Is he committing a sin? He's running a business, you get me? A business.'

'Yes, of course, and you're his paatnar.'

'I'm just supplying him rejas. These girls don't get enough to eat, I'm finding them jobs. What sin am I committing?'

'Thuu! I spit on your kind of work. You witch. You first became the malik's whore, and now you're making them whores too.'

'The blame lies elsewhere. Perhaps with you people. Why else would there be such poverty here?'

'Are you saying there's poverty because of us?'

'Oh ... I can't carry on arguing with you.'

'What else can you say?'

'Who's this girl?'

Shanichari, who had been gaping at them all this while, started. Hiralal spoke warningly, 'Don't look at her. Listen, girl! Call your grandmother or whoever she is. We've almost reached Tohri. And listen, if this Gohuman Bibi enters your village, drive her out.'

Gohuman smiled and said, 'We'll see. I've heard such threats before.'

'She's as poisonous as a cobra.'

---

[3] Gohuman: literally, a cobra.

'Huh ... look who's talking. Sings for his supper, and talks like a hero!'

Shanichari's grandmother suddenly woke up in the middle of all this. Immediately she began, 'And then the king said ...'

Shanichari said, 'We're almost there. Let's get off. No more stories.'

'We've reached?'

Gohuman Bibi had begun singing,

'Come with me, all you girls,

To Kolkatta we'll go,

Riding on a train,

Come on, off we go.'

The hustle and bustle of the Tohri haat started right at the station. Shanichari got off the train holding tight to her grandmother's hand. Hiralal too got down, playing his harmonium. Gohuman Bibi seemed to be looking for someone.

Shanichari walked hurriedly past Gohuman. She was scared of this woman.

'You, little girl,' Gohuman called out to her, 'Want a sweet?'

'No, no, I don't want anything.'

Oh baba! She's a spitting cobra! Did Shanichari want to die of snakebite? Writhing in pain?

But as luck would have it, Gohuman smuggled out a few girls from their village that very same year.

That year too there was a drought. A drought meant no harvest. Coarse paddy, gondli, maroa, uradh dal, sarguja—nothing came up. The earth cracked. Even the forest floor did not yield a thing. No roots, no tubers.

It was at such a time that Gohuman Bibi landed up at the Banki village haat. She gathered all the girls under a tree. Treated them to puris and laddus. Then she said, 'Know of any girls who'll come to Kolkatta? Work there as rejas in the brick kilns?'

The girls looked at each other.

'See if you can find me some girls.'

'What kind of work?'

'My malik is like a god. Since I usually take village girls like you who've never been to a city, he first makes sure they get to look around a bit, see the sights, have come fun. Then he gives them work at his brick kiln.'

'Don't the local girls want to work as rejas?'

'The Kolkatta girls? They wear chamak chamak saris, chhamak chhamak jewellery, prance around the place. Their homes are overflowing with puris and laddus. You think they'll work as rejas? Why should they?'

'Oh . . . !'

'You'll work four hours a day. Get ten rupees a day. Don't have to worry about where to stay, what to eat, how to buy clothes. The malik will take care of everything.'

'We'll come.'

'No, no, hang on. Go home, talk it over with your parents. If they agree, only then will I take you. I don't go in for shady deals. I'm a local girl myself. I come from Lalpur near the rail tracks.'

The pangs of an empty stomach are hard to resist. If they worked in the brick kilns of Kolkatta they'd get enough to eat, wear dazzling clothes and see the sights of the city. The girls explained this to their parents that night.

Gohuman Bibi talked to their parents, gave each of them fifty rupees in advance, made them put their thumbprints on blank paper and took the girls away.

Those four girls from Shanichari's village never came back. The city did not return them. What could Gohuman Bibi do? Apparently the girls were busy making pots of money. They were prancing around in chamak chamak saris, anklets, bracelets and necklaces going chhamak chhamak. They hardly remembered Dhurbaha village with its cracked red earth and dilapidated huts. Those young girls, once someone's daughter, someone's sister, had been lured away by the city of Kolkatta.

Their mothers would sing while drawing water from the well,

'I can hear the train whistling,

It took my girl away

To bake bricks in Kolkatta.'

Meanwhile, the little brothers they had left behind grew up and were soon old enough to go coal-gathering near the railway tracks. The saplings they had seen when they left the village had flowered into fruit-bearing trees. Sometimes there would be drought and the harvest would fail. At other times good rain would yield a rich crop. Slowly people began to forget those four girls. Who could remember forever those the city had taken away?

Mongru Oraon, too, never returned. Where was Kolkatta, where the brick kilns? Who could keep track of all this?

Shanichari came of age.

Shanichari was a big girl now. She was sixteen. Now she could go to the haats alone, both far and near. Her brothers were much younger. Shanichari was her parents' right hand. These days, like everybody else, she too took the mahajan's grains to the haat. The mahajan owned a lot of land, had a large granary. Dhurbaha was a very remote village. She could make some profit if she went to the big and busy haats. She earned two rupees a day.

One day Shanichari stopped short at the haat in Rata. Hiralal! His hair had greyed and he was wearing glasses. But it was definitely Hiralal. Playing his harmonium and singing.

Lo aa gaye unke yaad

Woh nahi aye.[4]

Shanichari stood there for a minute.

'Aren't you Moti Linda's daughter?'

---

[4] Lo aa gaye unke yaad/Woh nahi aye: literally 'The memory of them returns to me but they still stay away.'

'Yes.'

'That grandmother of yours?'

'She's dead.'

'What do you do?'

'Sell the mahajan's grain and pulses.'

'Good, good. Gohuman didn't get you?'

'No. Haven't seen her since then.'

'Oh, she'll be back. Last time, she took a few girls. Won't come for a few years. She's waiting for people to forget.'

'Then?'

'She'll lure new girls with promises of chamak chamak saris and chhamak chhamak jewellery.'

'Why don't the girls come back?'

'A monstrous city, Kolkatta. Devours everything around it—Ranchi-Singbhum-Palamau. Turns some girls into whores, sells off the rest.'

'Oh baba!'

That's what Gohuman does with her deadly fangs.

Two years later, Shanichari voluntarily gave herself up to Gohuman's fangs. She was all set to get married to Chand Tirkey that year.

That was when the Adi Jati Raksha Morcha movement swept through the countryside. And why not? The winds of change and forest fires could sweep through jungles equally rapidly. The Raksha Morcha was fighting for the rights of the adivasis. But Dhurbaha village and its environs witnessed no such struggle. The Morcha called a big meeting at the Rata village haat. Many joined in with their bows and arrows. And why shouldn't they? After all the Morcha had promised them a new azadi.[5]

---

[5] New azadi: Independence for the second time; economic independence, in the real sense.

'Sab julum bandh!'[6]

'The forest is ours!'

'No more felling trees!'

Parija Murmu had himself come to that meeting. And so had the police, lots of military police.

Later, no one could tell if it was the police who fired first or Murmu who ordered his men to shoot their arrows. After all, these men went everywhere with their bows and arrows. So it was quite natural to bring them to the meeting. Some people were heard saying that the police opened fire when they saw that the men were armed. A few of the military police were killed as well. And why wouldn't they be? Those who carry bows and arrows would obviously know how to use them.

All hell broke loose. People ran for cover to the primary health centre. The military police entered the clinic firing. Later a truck was brought in to carry away the corpses.

'Straight to the Mortongunj factory.'

'Quick! Throw the bodies into the furnace.'

'Take them away. Fast.'

'Eleven bodies. Only eleven to be left here.'

'Tell the press. Official figure eleven.'

That's how a small place like Rata suddenly made the headlines. And the military police was deployed in the region. Now there'd be no more newspaper reports. It was a question of prestige for the military police. 'Don't try to stop us, officer saab, don't make us revolt.'

'Once we do that, you'll lose all control.'

Today the public condemns the Bihar military misbehaviour. The moment the newspapers proclaim that the Bihar Military Police are 'revolutionaries', public opinion would immediately swing in their favour. Thanks to the Naxalite and the Jharkhand

---

[6] Sab julum bandh!: An end to oppression.

movements, a section of the public does have a soft spot for all 'revolutionaries'.

'Don't stop us. Leave the area to us.'

'This is the first time their arrows have struck the BMP.'

'BMP kills, tribals die. This time things were different.'

'Don't try to stop us.'

The officers said, 'Of course, of course, go ahead. We are BMP too. We want to be part of the action too.' They got into the act as well.

A state and a central minister came to find out things firsthand after being continuously pestered by the media. But the BMP didn't let them in either.

Rata was now declared a protected area. The word 'rata' meant 'red'. But BMP managed to turn red Rata into ranka. In other words, they stripped the place bare.

Which is why Shanichari felt the fangs of Gohuman.

You who have been reading this story must be wondering—so the Raksha Morcha meeting set things ablaze, guns went bang bang bang, dark-skinned men and women screamed and ran helter skelter, the white walls of the health centre were stained red by the BMP who removed all but eleven corpses, and proclaimed 'this is a prestige issue, we'll set the forest on fire'—but what does this have to do with Shanichari Linda, a lovely young Oraon girl, lush and lissom as the kusum tree?

You are also likely to think that this author is obsessed with issues like police–struggle–violence–adivasi–rakshamorcha and so on. That nothing else interests her.

But look, there's basically just the one question. Kaise bache? How does one survive? Well, this writer chose her path long ago—that of writing such stories. Asking herself what to write about, she trudged mile after mile down innumerable roads which all led to one destination. At the end she always stood face to face with battles, blood, sweat, tears. That's why I decided

Mahasweta Devi

to tell you Shanichari Linda's story.

The link between the Raksha Morcha meeting and Shanichari meeting Gohuman is both real and strong.

Did you ask why? Don't. You are intelligent, educated people. You know how such things work. Doesn't sugar cost you the earth because the sugar barons of north India pump a lot of money into donations, during elections? Even your morning cup of tea is intrinsically linked with the general elections in India.

Anyway, I'm not going to bore you with details of the sugar–coal–drugs nexus-plexus any further. Hats off to the government. It has hiked the price of essential commodities to help those who want higher profit margins, and made us realize that the saying 'Dilli door ast'[7] is nothing but lies. Actually Delhi is just around the corner. From lighting the stove every morning to stirring sugar in your tea—it's Delhi all the way.

Let me tell you the inside story. I've seen Shanichari with my own eyes. And for the past one year, Janum Singh has been writing to me regularly from Rata. Of course, people like you don't want to believe in my kind of true stories. You've got so used to make-believe tales that true stories don't attract you any longer.

Who's to blame for all this? Who's responsible?

Listen to Shanichari's story.

Once the police and the BMP took over Rata and its adjoining areas, there was no stopping them. Janum Singh wrote, 'The BMP, CRP and BSF[8] are combing the entire area and have unleashed a reign of terror. They are killing, torturing, plundering, destroying the crops in the field. It's inhuman.

[7] Dilli door ast: A proverbial expression literally meaning 'Delhi is a long way off' and implying that the task at hand is a long way from completion.
[8] CRP and BSF: The Central Reserve Police Force and the Border Security Force.

They've devoured all the poultry and goats. Smashed the ploughs. Destroyed whatever few possessions there were. Pots and pans, huts, all razed to the ground. The homeless adivasis have been driven to shelter in the forest. They have no rice, no salt. No clothes. They are hiding in the hills and forest caves. Families are split up, lost. No one knows where anyone is.'

You may have guessed by now that Janum Singh is a Bengali. I cannot disclose his identity. Besides, he's never wanted people to know who he is. You must be quite familiar with the long and lofty salutation to Sabyasachi in *Pather Dabi*.[9] I silently salute Janum Singh in a different kind of way. But this is not the time to wax lyrical about people like him. This is an hour of crisis. I just want you to know the meaning of his name. The work 'janum' means 'thorn' in the Ho tongue. This Janum Singh is a thorn for some people and to some others he's 'bah'—a flower.

Notice the phrase 'no clothes' in Janum's letter. Clothes—a whole new sari is a source of great empowerment. I know you'll realize this yourselves. How do I know this? Don't some of you buy saris worth thousands of rupees every Puja?

What else can I say? The reign of terror that was unleashed in Rata after the Raksha Morcha meeting continued unabated, forcing the young women to flee to the forest. They didn't have any clothes. The BMP had burnt down their huts along with the saris—coarse, white, multicoloured—that they had bought from the haat with the little money they had managed to earn after hours of back-breaking labour.

The BMP took the young girls into the forest and raped them. Imagine the scene. Familiar to you, no doubt, from innumerable story books—the lush green forest and a group of

---

[9] *Pather Dabi*: Saratchandra Chattopadhyay's famous Bengali novel, well-known to the middle-class reader.

Ho-Oraon-Munda girls who look as if they have been exquisitely carved out of black stone. Only the bestial howls of the BMP would have been left out of such a picture-book scene.

Without clothes, the girls are forced to hide in the forest. And it was at such a time that Gohuman Bibi appeared, like a veritable goddess. She told them, 'We'll get you new clothes and take you to Kolkatta to work in the brick kilns. You'll work hard, eat well, make money. Come, come!' Scores of young girls were bitten by Gohuman's fangs. There isn't just the one Gohuman, after all, hundreds of similar snakes are slithering around, now that they sense an opportunity. And it's easy for them to gain entry to the area.

The local police got a cut. The GRP,[10] too, got their share.

Of course, I cannot disclose the identities of all those who were bribed by Gohuman to turn a blind eye and pretend, 'We saw nothing, we heard nothing.' But I will not hesitate to state that if this last group of people had intervened, those girls could not have been smuggled out so easily.

Shanichari went with them.

Oh, did I not mention that Chand Tirkey was amongst those shot dead by the police at the Rata meeting, his body loaded onto a truck and carted off to be burnt in the furnace?

Shanichari had loved Chand. On the run from the BMP, she would remember Chand and realize that her emotions were burnt to ashes. Of course, everything may burn to cinders but the pangs of hunger refuse to die. The forest provided enough roots and tubers for them to survive on. But the forest could not provide them cloth to hide their shame.

Which is why Shanichari felt Gohuman's fangs. And in house after house, dark-skinned, grieving mothers sang,

---

[10] GRP: General Railway Police.

'My girl could live on tubers,
Wear leafs and buds in her ears,
Alas, trees can't grow clothes
"Dear Ma," my girl said, "So
To the brick kilns I must go
To the brick kilns I must go."'

They took the night train to Howrah. From there, a bus ride to the Shyambazar five-point crossing. Then to Barasat, to Rahmat Sardar's 'Taraknath'-brand brick kiln. You must, of course, know how very little it costs to run a brick kiln and how very high the profits are. Which is why people like Rahmat, Irfan or Shiulal from north Bihar have opened these kilns in and around Kolkatta. They force the poor small farmers to give up their land by offering them money or by terrorizing them through local musclemen.

Thereafter the neighbouring farmer voluntarily sells off his land at a throwaway price. And why shouldn't he? His land becomes a public thoroughfare for the coolies and labourers working in the adjoining brick kiln. His crops are destroyed. So he sells off his land.

After all, people like you are busy building your houses—big houses, small houses, dream houses, foreign picture-book houses, matchbox flats, skyscraper office buildings and what not. Brick piled upon brick.

Due to the searing temperature of the furnace, the soil around a brick kiln becomes barren for a few hundred years. But that's none of your business. Let the paddy fields go. What have you got to do with paddy, after all? You're a rice eater.

Shanichari and the others reached Rahmat's brick kiln in mid-September. Yes, the kilns run from mid-September, just after the rains, to mid-June, the onset of the monsoons. Three months shut. Nine months open.

The wall surrounding the brick kiln was as high as a jail wall.

Mahasweta Devi

Inside were Rahmat and his goons' pucca houses. Rahmat inspected all the girls thoroughly. Then he escorted them to Indrapuri.[11]

A row of pigsties. Walls of palm leaf thatched with coconut leaves. Shanichari's throat went dry at the sight. She asked for some water.

A single tubewell. One tubewell for three hundred people.

Rahmat ordered, 'Out with your names. All of you bastards. You there, start.'

'Shanichari Linda. Father Moti Linda. Village Dhurbaha. P.S. Rata.'

'You dumb idiot, have you written it down?'

'Yes, huzoor.'

'Read it out.'

'Somni Oraon. Father Kormu Oraon. Village Baheria. P.S. Lohardaga.'

'Well done. Listen, you bunch of animals. No one will ever be able to trace you here. So there's no point in trying to talk to anyone on the outside. You work, you get paid every week. No off-days. Now listen . . .'

They listened.

'After working here nine months you'll realize you were better off with the BMP.'

'Ai baba!'

'Hah! The rejas will carry the bricks, the patariyas will place them, the labourers will dig the ground and the rubbishmen will handle the kiln. Go it?'

'Huzoor.'

'You'll carry unbaked bricks in piles of ten. Each time, my munshi will give you a tikli. After you've carried 210 bricks and got 21 tiklis, you earn a rupee. Baked bricks will also be carried

---

[11] Indrapuri: Abode of Indra, the King of Gods, lived in Indrapuri, famed for its magnificent architecture.

in piles of ten. After you've got 44 tiklis for 440 bricks, you'll make a rupee. Now go. Eat your roti-sabji and go to sleep.'

They looked at each other in shocked silence. Are they now prisoners in this alien land under these alien circumstances?

'Go, go. Move.'

They had begun to move. Suddenly Shanichari said, 'We won't work here. Send us back.'

'Indeed. And who'll pay your train fare?'

'Train fare? We travelled without tickets thanks to the bribe you paid the police.'

'Oh, ho! Quite a girl, this! Will you be able to find your way back home?'

'We'll ask people.'

'So you want to leave? Look there.'

The gates were locked. The girls cried out in fright. Rahmat gestured to his men to drag the girls away. He grabbed Shanichari by the hand, saying, 'Come, share some meat curry and rice with me. You're just my type. Spunky girls like you are more fun.'

Shanichari Linda's scream was cut off by Rahmat. His men continued pushing the other girls around.

Shanichari didn't find out what life was like as an ordinary reja. But her companions did. Joshima, Lugri, Jhini, Parai and Phulmani faced the worst. You work all day in the kilns. No matter how many bricks you actually carry, you get not more than fifteen rupees a week. The rest of your earnings are deposited as chapayia with the employer. To be given to you when you return home.

From that fifteen rupees you buy a weeks' ration of rice and salt. Eat rice or rice water mixed with salt and green chillies. Tea, khaini, oil, all come out of that money.

At the end of the day, when you're too tired to keep your eyes open, the head mastaan will call out your name in the daily auction. Today you go to him, tomorrow the driver, the

Mahasweta Devi

day after the munshi.

You don't get holidays for the Pujas or for the festival of Holi. The owner doesn't care what the labour laws in Bihar or West Bengal are. Why should he, tell me? Why indeed? With the local police, mafia, in his pocket, he can't be bothered.

At home in the village, you are used to celebrating the spring with Sarjombah, welcoming the new leaves and budding flowers.

But here you're petrified of Holi. The malik's friends arrive in hordes from Kolkatta. They force liquor down your throat till you pass out. Pull off your clothes. What happens next only your body knows.

Shanichari, of course, didn't have to pay such a heavy price. She belonged to Rahmat.

She would spit at the Gohumans when she saw them.

Gohuman would say, 'I was once a reja like you.'

'Thuu!Thuu! Thuu!'

'Who's to blame for all this? Who?'

Rahmat would dress Shanichari in good clothes and nice jewellery, rub fragrant oil in her hair—and then tear into her ruthlessly.

When Shanichari began throwing up one day, Rahmat said, 'From tomorrow you'll work as a reja. Josin will stay here with me. Lug bricks, get paid.'

Lug bricks, lug bricks, Shanichari. You wonder where you are, where you've been brought—you can't quite figure out where this place is. With Rahmat's child in your womb, you stare blankly at the paddy fields stretching to the horizon. The endless fields beckon you to freedom, but you know you're a prisoner. You don't know the local language, nor do you remember the way here.

If you were carrying Chand Tirkey's child, your people would have accepted it. But how can you return home with a diku's child in your womb? In your mind's eye the paddy fields turn into the sal forest, the narrow path between the fields becomes an undulating hill track, and the quiet village in the distance into Dhurbaha.

Then one day the brick kiln shut down. Nobody got the chapaiya deposited with the employer. Rahamat handed a new janta sari and a train ticket to each girl and sent them all home.

Shanichari too wore a new sari and, clutching a ticket, climbed on to the truck. All the other girls had also been abused, but she was the only one returning with a child in her womb. Gohuman had given the others pills.

When the train reached Chakradharpur, what a coincidence—Hiralal! Singing, Lo aa gaye unke yaad; and Shanichari burst into tears as soon as she heard him.

No, Shanichari Linda wasn't accepted in their village. What could they do? They lived their lives as victims of the dikus. How could their priest, the naiga, allow a woman carrying a diku's child to be accepted in society?

Moti Linda, Shanichari's father said, 'I'll pay for a repentance feast.'

'Why should you? Is it Shanichari's fault?' asked Chand Tirkey's elder brother.

'That's the norm,' said their naiga.

The repentance rites and the feast were held.

Nevertheless, Shanichari remained an outcast. Her son was born. No, they didn't ask her to abandon the child. The Ho–Oraon–Munda–Santhals loved children.

Her parents asked, 'What will you do now?'

'You tell me.'

Shanichari was unable to think clearly for a long time. She would sit with her back to the wall and stare dully into the distance.

One day she bestirred herself. Sat up and said, 'Ma?'

'Yes?'

'Remember the four girls who never returned from the brick kiln?'

'Of course I do.'

'They were sold off.'

'Who sold them?'

'Malik.'

'Sold them?'

'Of course. They are sold off, turned into whores, made pregnant like me.'

'It's our destiny.'

'My son will never get married, Ma.'

'Why worry about that now?'

'Such boys can only get married to such girls. That's the khawasin custom.'

'That's true.'

'How we despised them.'

'Don't think about it.'

'Don't want to. But I can't help it.'

'We're here for you, aren't we?'

'Ma, help me build a room for myself.'

'We will.'

'You look after the baby. I'll gather coal near the rail tracks and sell it.'

'He's still nursing.'

'I'll carry him on my back.'

They put up a room for her. Walls of tree branches. Thatched with leaves. She cooked separately, ate alone.

Chand Tirkey's brother said, 'We should think about this as a community. There could be more Shanicharis in the future. Should we cast out our own women? Will that benefit our society?'

The naiga said, 'We'll think about it later.'

Shanichari didn't blame her people or ask any questions. She began collecting coal with her son strapped to her back. One day, after selling off the coal, she was buying some oil and salt. Suddenly she stopped short at the sight of Hiralal.

'Hiralal!'

'Yes?'

'Why won't you look at me?'

'What will I see?'

Shanichari smiled. Soothing him, she said, 'Gohuman Bibi too is not the real culprit. You didn't know that. But I've realized it.'

'Then who is, Shanichari? Who?'

'Everything around you, ev-er-y-thing.' Shanichari stretched out her arms to include the world around her, standing stock still.

I know Shanichari is showing us who the real culprits are. I also know that she's waiting.

But I do not know how long she'll have to wait. Her story is not over. As long as people like Rahmat unabashedly run brick kilns, as long as Gohumans entice girls like Shanichari, till our motherland can provide basic food and clothing to girls like her, the freeze shot of Shanichari pointing her finger at the accused will remain.

— *Translated from the Bangla by Sarmistha Dutta Gupta*

Phakirmohan Senapathy

Rebati

Patpur, a nondescript village, was tucked away in one corner of Hariharpur pargana, in the district of Cuttack. In the furthest corner of the village stood Shyambandhu Mohanty's house. It had four rooms, arranged in two rows, a rice-husking shed, a courtyard with a well, a veranda in the front and a vegetable corner in the backyard. Visitors were entertained in the outer room and the farmers who came to clear their tax dues also assembled there. Shyambandhu Mohanty, the zamindar's accountant, was entrusted with the task of collecting rent. His salary was two rupees a month, and a little more came his way by updating rent receipts and land records. He earned a total of four rupees a month with which he managed, somehow, to make ends meet. In fact, he was quite comfortable. No one in his house complained of lacking anything. Besides a vegetable patch in the backyard, there were two drumstick trees and he also had two cows, so there was always some milk and curd in the kitchen. They hardly ever bought firewood, as Shyambandhu's old mother mixed cow-dung and husk to make fuel cake. The zamindar had given him three and half acres of land for cultivation. The crop was just enough for them, never more or less.

Shyambandhu was a straightforward person and the tenants respected and liked him. He went from door to door, coaxing them to pay their rents in time, but never forced anyone to pay so much as an extra paisa. The tenants never had to ask him for the receipts. He always came himself and stuck the four-finger-wide palm leaf receipts in the thatch of their houses. He prevented the zamindar's muscleman from entering the village—he'd stroke the fellow's chin and lead him by the hand, all the while tucking two paise for tobacco into the waistfolds of his cloth. Shyambandhu had four mouths to feed at home—he and his wife, his old mother, and his ten-year-old daughter, Rebati. In the evenings, Shyambandhu sat in the veranda and sang 'Krupasindhu Badan' and other prayer-songs; at times he balanced an oil lamp on a wooden stand and read aloud portions from the Bhagawat. Rebati sat close by and listened attentively. Very soon, she learnt a few verses by heart. Her childish recital made the prayer-songs more appealing. People from the surrounding houses would come to listen to her. There was one particular bhajan that was Shyambandhu's favourite. Every evening he asked Rebati to sing it and she sang in a lilting voice,

'To whom shall I address my pleas,

If you don't look my way, Lord,

Surely my end is near.

Whether you save me or not,

I have offered my life at your feet

Your name is imprinted in my heart.

All three worlds are empty

Without you, Oh Lord Hari!

Only the potion of your love,

Can calm my life, my Hari!'

Two years ago, during his rural tour, the Deputy Inspector of schools had spent a night at Patpur. On the request of some prominent village elders, he had got approval from the Inspector of schools of Orissa Division, and established an upper primary school in the village. The teacher's salary was four rupees a month, which was paid by the government. Apart from this, each student paid an anna every month. The teacher, Basudev, had passed the teachers' training course at the Cuttack Normal School. True to his name he had striking good looks and a pleasant disposition. Polite and humble, he never looked directly at anyone while walking down the village road. His inherent goodness was reflected in his calm exterior. Basudev was around twenty years old. As a reminder of his mother's attempts to cure him of an attack of diphtheria when he was still a child, there was the unmistakable imprint of the heated mouth of a bottle on his forehead. This enhanced his appeal. Orphaned at an early age, Basudev had grown up in the care of his uncle. He belonged to Shyambandhu's caste.

Sometimes, on a Thursday or on a full moon, when rice cakes and sweets were prepared at home, Shyambandhu, who had taken a liking to Basudev, would go to the school and invite him to their house: 'Son Basu, your auntie wants you to come to our place this evening.' These visits had forged a bond of affection between them. Even Rebati, in her concern, would sometimes remark, 'Ah, the poor orphan! Who's there to give him food—what does he eat?' Almost every evening, Basu visited Shyambandhu and spent some time with him. Rebati would spot him approaching the house and chant, 'Basu bhai is here, Basu bhai is here.' Then she would sit beside her father and sing all the devotional songs she had memorized. For Basu, the songs were always fresh and new.

One day, Shyambandhu learnt that there was a school in Cuttack, where girls could study and train in crafts as well. From that day, Shyambandhu nursed the desire to educate Rebati. He sought Basu's advice on the matter. Basu, who regarded Shyambandhu as a father, said, 'I was about to suggest it myself.' Both of them agreed that Rebati should be sent to Cuttack to study. Rebati, who had been listening intently to the entire conversation, leaped indoors to convey the good tidings to her mother and grandmother. 'I am going to study,' she announced merrily. 'I will learn to read and write.' Her mother was very happy for her, but her grandmother retorted, 'How will studies help you, silly girl? Rather, you should learn how to cook, prepare savouries, make butter and decorate walls with floral patterns.'

At night, when Shyambandhu sat on a mango wood stool eating his dinner, with Rebati sitting close to him, the old lady sat in front of them issuing orders to her daughter-in-law: 'Get some more rice, soak it with some dal, bring a bit of salt.' Then suddenly, she asked her son, 'Shyam, dear! Will Rebi really go away to study? How will reading help a girl?'

'Well,' Shyambandhu said, 'if she wants to, I will let her. Don't you know, Jhankad Pattnaik's daughters can read and recite from the Bhagawat and *Vaidehisha Vilas*?' An incensed Rebati turned on her grandmother. 'Go away, old hag,' she shouted. She implored her father, 'I want to study.' 'Yes, you definitely will,' replied Shyambandhu, and the matter ended there.

Basudev got a copy of Sitanathbabu's *First Lessons* for Rebati the next evening. Her joy knew no bounds as she scanned the book from cover to cover. She was fascinated with the pictures of elephants, horses and cows. Kings regarded elephants and horses as prized possessions in their stables, others enjoyed riding them, but the pictures were enough to mesmerize Rebi. She ran to her mother to show the pictures.

Her irate grandmother said, 'Oh, get lost.'

'Stupid old woman,' Rebati yelled back.

The following day was Sripanchami, an auspicious day to begin lessons. Early in the morning, Rebati took her bath, wore new clothes, and roamed around the house impatiently, awaiting Basu's arrival. The customary fanfare of the 'initiation ceremony' had been dispensed with for fear of her grandmother's ire. Basu arrived a little after ten in the morning and taught her the alphabets: a, aa, e, ee, oo, ooo ...

The lessons continued over the next two years. Rebati made good progress with her lessons during this time. She didn't falter even once while reciting Madhu Rao's poems.

One night, Shyambandhu sat talking to his mother over dinner. It seemed they were finalizing a matter they had been discussing earlier.

Shyambandhu asked, 'So, Ma, what is your opinion?'

'It is ideal,' the old lady said, 'but what about his caste?'

'What do you think I was doing all these days? So what if he is poor, he comes from a good Karan family.'

'It is not wealth, but caste which is the deciding factor. But will he stay with us?'

'Why should he want to go elsewhere? His uncle and aunt are the only relatives he has.'

Rebati alone knew what she made out from the conversation. But it brought about a marked change in her behaviour. She felt shy when Basu came to teach her, smiled without reason, and hung her head low to suppress her giggles. She did not read the lessons aloud and answered in monosyllables. As soon as the lessons were over for the day, she rushed inside shaking with ripples of laughter. Every evening, she would stand by the front door, scanning the road, as if she were waiting for someone. But the moment Basu came, she disappeared inside.

Another Sripanchami went by to mark the end of two years. But, in the Lord's scheme of things, no two days are the same. On a bright Phalgun day, a cholera epidemic struck the village without the slightest warning. The rumour that Shyambandhu had been afflicted with cholera buzzed around the village. In villages, people respond to such news by shutting all the doors and windows of their houses, as though the disease were an old hag, roaming around with a basket to collect human heads. Not a soul dared to step out. The two women in the house, Shyambandhu's wife and his mother, were helpless. Rebati ran about wildly, calling for help. When Basudev heard the news, he rushed to their house. He sat beside Shyambandhu without a trace of fear or care for his life, stroking his hands and legs and feeding him drops of water. After three hours, Shyambandhu suddenly looked at Basu, his eyes wide open, and stammered, 'Take care of my Reba.' Basu could not hold back his tears. The house was in a turmoil. Rebati rolled on the floor in despair. As evening approached, Shyambandhu passed away.

A thousand arrangements had to be made for the cremation. They were too numb with grief to think clearly about what they should do. It was Bana Sethi, the village washerman, who had helped arrange several cremations, who rose to the occasion. Bana came to the house with a towel tied around his waist and an axe slung over his shoulder. Theirs was the only Karan family in the entire village and the devastated family members gathered together to perform the last rites. It was dawn by the time they returned from the cremation ground. The moment they reached home, Rebati's mother was struck by cholera and by noon, succumbed to it. The entire village lamented the misfortune.

Time doesn't wait for anyone; on some it bestows the cool shade of the royal umbrella, on some other, whiplashes on fettered feet. But it flows by. Three months had passed since Shyambandhu's sudden death. The zamindar had taken possession of Shyambandhu's cows to compensate for the last rent collection that Shyambandhu had not deposited. No one in the village believed this. Everybody knew that Shyambandhu could not rest in peace till he had deposited every single rupee he had collected in the zamindar's treasury. The zamindar had actually coveted the cows for a long time. He also withdrew the land he had given Shyambandhu for cultivation. The farmhand, now idle, left on the day of the full moon. Rebati and her grandmother had sold the pair of cows in the market for seventeen and half rupees. After meeting the funeral expenses, they managed for a month with the amount that was left. In the days that followed, they had to depend on pawning items: a brass bowl some day, a plate the next.

Basu looked them up twice a day, and left late in the night at bedtime. They had consistently refused Basu's repeated offers to give them some money. Sometimes, when he forced it on them, it remained untouched, unused. Basu realized he had failed to convince them in this matter. So, every now and then, he took the money grandmother gave and bought provisions for the house. The straw roof of the house needed repair. Basu had bought some straw with two rupees. But, despite all his efforts, the roof couldn't be thatched.

Grandmother had stopped lamenting her misfortune day and night as she used to before. Now, it was in the evenings that she gave vent to her grief. Weak and worn out after crying, she would collapse on the floor and spend the entire night like that. Rebati would lie close by trembling with suppressed sobs all through the night. Mad with grief, Grandmother had lost her bearings. Her vision was not clear. However, her bouts of crying had lessened and, instead, she hurled curses at Rebati. She firmly believed that Rebati was the reason for all her sorrow and misery. Her education had been the biggest mistake and had triggered all the mishaps—the death of her son and daughter-in-law, the farmhand deserting them, the cows being sold, the zamindar taking away the cows, and the loss of her eye-sight. Rebati was the illomen, the devil, the curse.

During these fierce tirades, Rebati would withdraw in fear to some corner of the house, tears flooding her cheeks. She would hide her face and sit still, like a block of stone.

Basu was equally to blame, raved Grandmother. All these days, Rebati had not studied. It was Basu who had initiated it. But she was careful not to reveal her thoughts to Basu, as she was completely dependent on him. The zamindar continued to send his messengers to collect papers or details of accounts, and only Basu could easily find the documents among Shyambandhu's stack of papers.

Rebati was no more the bright lamp that lit up the house. She never uttered a word or stepped out of the house. She no longer wailed loudly. Her eyes shimmered constantly with unshed tears like blue lilies floating in water. Her heart and mind had been shattered. Day and night seemed alike to her. The sun had no light, the night no darkness and there was emptiness all around. She was obsessed with thoughts of her parents. Their memories and images flitted before her eyes unceasingly. She could not come to terms with their death; with the fact that they had gone, never to return. She seemed to have no desire to eat or sleep. A burning need for her parents consumed her. Her skin hung loose on the bones. Thin as a reed and malnourished, she did not have the strength to raise herself from the floor where she lay curled up. Only Basudev's visits instilled some life in her. Her eyes glued on him, she would lower her head with a sigh only when their glances met. She would desperately find ways to look at him again, as long as he was around. He encompassed everything then, her eyes, her mind, her heart.

Five months had now gone by. On a blazing summer afternoon, Basu knocked on their door. He had never visited them before at this hour. Grandmother dragged herself to the door and opened it.

'Grandma,' Basu said, 'the Deputy Inspector of schools will take an oral test of the students in the Hariharpur police station. All the schools will send their students. I got the letter today. I will leave with the students tomorrow morning. It will be five days before I return.'

Rebati was standing behind the door. Her legs gave way and she sank to the ground when she heard this. She narrowly missed getting seriously hurt as she had a grip on the door.

Basu bought rice, salt, oil and some brinjals for them for the next five days, sought Grandmother's blessings and prepared to leave.

'Son,' Grandmother croaked, 'don't be out in the sun for long. Take care of yourself. Have your food on time.'

Then she sighed heavily.

Rebati's intent stare followed Basu. Today, she didn't avert her gaze when he looked, but gazed deep into his eyes. There was a difference in Basu's gaze as well.

Earlier, despite an irresistible longing to look at Rebati, he could not. A few furtive glances was all he could manage. But today, he couldn't tear his eyes away from her. They shared a deep and intimate glance that conveyed much more than before.

The inky darkness of the evening enveloped the house, the roads and everything else around. Rebati still stood, staring at the road, till Grandmother's call jolted her back to her senses.

Everyday, Rebati counted the minutes, willing Basu to return. Since her parents' death, she had never been near the front door. But, on the sixth day, she was involuntarily drawn towards it. At about ten in the morning, the students returned from Hariharpur with the shocking news of Basu's demise. He had been afflicted by cholera and had breathed his last under the big banyan tree in Gopalpur. The village folk were grief-stricken; the women and children wept. 'How handsome he was,' some said. 'And so gentle,' others remarked, 'so kind, he wouldn't hurt a fly.'

Grandmother choked on her sobs. 'Alas! Son,' she whispered, 'you asked for it.' In her mind, Basu's death was retribution for his foolish attempt to educate Rebati.

Ever since she heard the news, Rebati had been in a death-like trance. The next morning, Grandmother couldn't find Rebati nearby and shouted, 'You, Rebati! Hey, Rebi! You hell-fire, you ashbin!' The old lady's grief was transformed into anger. Passers-by and neighbours often heard, 'You Rebati! Hey, Rebi! You hell-fire, you ashbin!' Grandmother groped around the whole house. When she finally stumbled upon Rebati, a cold fear crept into her. Rebati, who was unconscious, had a raging fever. Sick with worry, she touched her hands. It was as if fire was coursing through Rebati's veins. Her mind searched for who she could turn to in this crisis. There was no one. Frantic and desperate, she retorted, 'What medicine can there be for an illness that you invite upon yourself?' In Grandmother's eyes, it was Rebati's foray into studying that had resulted in all the misfortune.

Five days passed. Rebati hadn't risen from the floor. Her eyes were shut, not even a groan escaped her lips. It was only on the morning of the sixth day that Rebati called out weakly. Grandmother went close, her hand stroking Rebati's body. The fever had gone down. Her hands and legs were cold. Rebati stared feverishly, and mumbled incoherently. Even a village quack could have diagnosed thus: 'Thirst, fever, incoherence, these are the symptoms of death.' But, Grandmother felt assured —by God's grace, the fever had gone down, and Rebi was able to open her eyes and speak a few words. She even had water after six whole days. These were signs of definite improvement. A little food and Rebati would be up and about.

'Take rest,' said Grandmother, 'I will cook something for you.' But all the pots and pans in the house were empty. She could not find even a handful of rice. In despair, she sighed and sat down. If she had better vision, she would have realized that the provisions bought for five days had already lasted for ten.

Yet, there was a faint glimmer of hope. She groped around

and found an old brass bowl. It had a hole in the bottom but she could pawn it. She started for Hari Shah's shop. He stocked rice, dal, salt and oil which he sold to the village folk and passers-by. The moment he saw the brass bowl in her hand, he realized she had come asking for food. He waited for her to speak and then examined the brass bowl minutely. 'There is no stock of rice,' he said. 'Do you think this old, cracked bowl, will fetch you anything?' This was just a ploy for a better bargain and Hari Shah had both the stock of rice and the desire to sell it.

The old lady was dumbfounded, as though struck by lightning. What would she feed Rebati? The girl was too weak and needed to eat. She sat there, brooding, not aware of the passing hours. Every now and then she'd look at the shopkeeper. Suddenly, she remembered Rebi. She had been away a long time. She rose to her feet and retraced her steps. As she stooped down to pick up the bowl, Hari Shah said, 'All right, give me the bowl. Let me see what I can manage.' He gave her a handful of rice and a sprinkling of cereals and salt. The old lady's laboured pace was ever so slow as she returned home. It was as if she rested more than she walked. Her mind was in such turmoil that she hadn't even brushed her teeth since the morning. She called out to Rebati as she reached home. She prayed that the girl was better. Then she would ask her to draw water from the well and she would cook the rice. Infuriated at the silence that welcomed her, she yelled, 'Rebati! You hell-fire! You ashbin!'

Rebati was in a critical condition by now: a searing pain was tearing at her limbs, her body was turning cold. She was thirsty and her tongue was dry. She felt her tongue being pulled back into her throat. The room was hot and stifling and she wanted to be where it was cool. She dragged herself to the inner courtyard. But she found no relief and wriggled out to the veranda. It was a windy evening. She sat leaning against the wall. She looked at the vegetable patch they had. The banana tree her father had planted just last year was laden with fresh bunches of bananas. She saw the guava tree her mother had planted so tenderly two years back. She remembered how she had run to the well and back again with a jug full of water for the plant. It had now grown tall and was bedecked with blossoms. Suddenly, memories of her mother engulfed her. Thoughts were jumbled in her mind and she couldn't find a sequence. But, through all this, her mother's image remained etched in her mind. It was well past evening. Darkness streamed out from amidst the branches of the tree and filled the backyard. She looked up at the sky. The evening star shone with a bright glitter. Rebati stared unblinkingly at the star. As she gazed, it grew steadily bigger and brighter, a circular form that covered the whole sky. And lo! Her mother's loving face filled the star, beckoning to her, to enter her world of love and kindness. She extended her shining arms towards her. The two shafts of light touched her eyes and spilled over into her heart. Her laboured breathing was the only sound in the stillness all around. Gradually, the breathing accelerated, like a steady groan until she whispered her mother's name twice. Then, a deadly silence fell on the surroundings.

The old lady had been all over the house, searching for Rebati—the bedroom, the veranda, the rice-husking shed—but she was not to be found. She felt then that with the fever gone, Rebati might be in the backyard, taking a walk. Her call was unmistakable, 'Hey Rebati! You hell-fire, you ashbin!' She climbed up to the veranda, which was a narrow ledge, and was shocked when she bumped into Rebati. 'So here you are,' she exclaimed, but fear coursed through her as she touched Rebati. She groped around, feeling Rebati, touching her from head to toe, then she held a hand under Rebi's nose. A wild wail escaped her lips. It was followed by the sound of bodies falling from the veranda.

No one has ever seen the family members of Shyambandhu Mohanty since that night, but neighbours remember clearly the refrain they heard in the wee hours of that fateful night—'You, Rebati! You hell-fire! You ashbin!'

— *Translated from the Oriya by Adyasha Das*

Mrinal Pande

Girls

The day we left with Ma for Naani's house, Baabu broke a surahi. I don't know whether he did it on purpose or by accident, but anyway the floor was flooded with water. Ma held up her sari and called Saru's mother—who was trying to eavesdrop from the adjacent room—to mop up the water, because if someone were to slip and break their bones it would be yet another problem. To Ma, everything in life is a problem. As far as she is concerned, whether we are at home or at school, ill or just playing around, we are a problem. While mopping the floor, Saru's mother looked up at Ma and asked, 'This time you'll be away for at least three months, won't you?' Ma put her hands on her thighs as if she were assessing their weight, squatted down and said, 'Yes, they won't allow me to come back sooner.' She turned to me and ordered me to go out and play. I always seemed to turn up at the wrong time and at the wrong place. As I was leaving the room I managed to pick up a piece of the broken surahi which I enjoyed sucking, and I overheard Ma addressing either Saru's mother or the cobwebs hanging from the roof: 'I hope it's a boy this time. It will relieve me of the nuisance of going through another pregnancy.' I could just imagine Saru's mother, in her usual manner, shaking her head and saying, 'Why not? ... why not?'

When we reached the station, I scrambled on to the train, fought my way through people and luggage and secured a place next to the window. Triumphantly I stuck my tongue out at everyone and went 'Eee ... Eee.' But when I noticed Ma's gaze turning towards me, I immediately started chanting the alphabet, 'E for imli, ee for eekh.' Ma was not actually looking at me though, because she was preoccupied with all her problems. She had to mind the luggage, the wobbling surahi, the three of us, and cope with the exhaustion of pregnancy as well. At one of the stations we bought a lot of samosas filled with chillies. Just when we were buying them, a woman was making her child pee through the next window. The sight made me feel quite nauseous and I couldn't eat my samosa, so I gave it to Ma instead. Meanwhile I crushed a piece of potato which was lying on the seat into the shape of an insect to frighten my younger sister. She screamed, Ma smacked me and I started to cry as well. My elder sister was irritated and said, 'Oh what a nuisance you are!' Despite her irritation, I know that it is only my elder sister who really loves me; everyone else is horrible.

Maama was waiting to receive us at the station. On the way to Naani's I sat next to Maami and noticed the rubies in her earlobes bobbing up and down while she chewed paan. Every time the driver pressed the jeep's horn, my sisters and I would scream in unison, 'Poo-poo'. The driver was amused at our screaming, and when we reached the house, he lifted me and my younger sister out of the jeep. He had a huge moustache, smelt of tea and bidis, and wore a uniform made of coarse wool which tickled me and made me feel sleepy. When the surahi was lifted out of the jeep it overturned, and once again there was water everywhere. This incident reminded me so much of Baabu that, absent-mindedly, I trod hard on my younger sister's sandal, nearly tripping her up. 'You are the cause of all my problems!' Ma hissed at me through tightly clenched teeth so that no one could hear. She then grabbed hold of my arm as if to prevent me from falling over but actually pressed it so hard that my shoulder hurt.

I thought of Baabu because whenever we came to Naani's house, he never accompanied us. And as soon as we arrived, Ma would be lost in the company of maasis, maamis, Naani and old maid-servants. If we tried going near her during the day, someone or other would say, 'Let the poor thing have some rest at least while she is here.' Ma too would put on a pathetic act as if we always harassed her at home. I felt disgusted at the thought of entering Naani's house, so I deliberately loitered behind near the bushes. A mongrel dog came near and sniffed at me. Then I heard someone mentioning my name inside the house and saying, 'Now where has she disappeared?'

I entered the house along with the dog and saw Naani sitting with Maama's son on her lap. As soon as she saw the dog, she shooed it away because to her all animals were untouchables. The dog, used to being reprimanded, tucked its tail between its legs and went out. I was told to bend down and touch Naani's feet. Someone from the family said, 'Not like that ... bend properly. You are born a girl and you will have to bend for the rest of your life, so you might as well learn.' Naani blessed me by waving her hand over my bowed back and said, 'This girl hasn't grown taller. Who would believe she is eight years old?'

Even though I pinched Maama's son, he kept following me around like an idiot. He was very fair, chubby and supposed to be cute. He was also tall for his age, and though only five years old could easily pass for seven. 'Will you tell me a story tonight?' he asked. I said no and pretended to read the newspaper.

'Oh what a nuisance this is,' Ma kept complaining. The old lady from the neighbourhood who had come to see Ma told Naani, 'This time Lali will definitely have a boy. Just look at her complexion—when she was expecting the girls it was pink, but now it has a tinge of yellow. I am sure it will be a boy this time.'

'Who knows, perhaps even this time ...,' moaned Ma as she put on a pathetic expression and began paring her nails.

'Is there anyone to cook for your husband?' asked the old lady. Her question set me thinking about Baabu, how good he smelt and the softness of his lap. And how when we came here Ma did not allow us to lie in her lap for too long and complained, 'Ugh! Oh! My bones are aching, my sari is all crushed. Get up now. I have such a lot of work to do, and to top it all there's this huge nuisance. Come on, get up.'

Naani folds her hands and prays: 'Oh goddess, protect my honour. At least this time let her take a son back from her parents' home.' At the end of the prayer she dries her tears with her pallav.

From the corner of my eyes I could see that my sisters were fast asleep. We were in a big room divided into two by a wooden partition. Right above my bed hung a big wall clock which was ticking away. Just before it struck the hour it made a hissing noise which was similar to my sister drawing in her breath just before howling. All the lights had been switched off and the room was flooded with moonlight. Tulsa dai was applying oil to the soles of Ma's feet and saying, 'If it's a boy this time, I will demand a sari with stainless steel zari.' Even in the bright moonlight I could not see Ma's face, but only her huge stomach which looked like a drum. Ma's sari had slipped down and Tulsa dai while feeling her stomach touched a painful spot which made Ma moan just like a cow does when returning home from the fields.

'If I have a boy this time, then I will be relieved of this burden forever,' she tells Tulsa dai, and then adds, 'you can go home now, your children must be waiting for you. Be sure you put the oil vessel under the bed, otherwise one of these kids will kick it over in the morning and ...' Ah, a bad omen. Whenever Ma left a sentence unfinished it seemed to loom in the air, like the ticking of the clock. I wonder why grown-ups always complete their sentences when they are talking about pleasant things, but always leave them unfinished if it's something unpleasant. Like, 'Ah, a woman's fate ...,' or 'Oh, three girls ...' There's always a silence after these half-statements.

There's a bright star in the sky. Is that the Dhruva star? Baabu used to say that if I worked hard I could become anything I wanted, just as Dhruva became a star. 'But I can't become a boy, can I?' I once asked obstinately. I was surprised at Baabu's reaction when he put on a serious look and said sternly, 'Don't argue with your elders now.' I find it difficult to understand them. My elder sister says one should never trust grown-ups because if they want to know something they will prise it out of you by hook or by crook, but they themselves will never tell you a thing.

It's true, nobody ever tells us anything. In this place, it's when we go to sleep that the world of the elders awakens, opening like a magic casket. I want to stay awake and listen; I don't know why I fall asleep half-way through. I wonder whose voice it is now; it sounds as if someone is crying in suppressed tones. Is it Chhoti Maasi? 'I don't even get as much respect as a dog does in that house,' she tells Ma. I wonder where she is treated worse than a dog, then I hear Ma telling her, 'All of us suffer like that, one just has to endure it.' My eyes shut and I fall asleep.

The next morning, when everyone is having breakfast I ask Ma what 'endure' means. I remind her by asking, what does Chhoti Maasi have to endure? I get one light slap, then another, but before Ma strikes me again Maami saves me and says, 'Let it be. She's only a child, after all.' 'She's always listening on the sly to elders talking. Heaven knows what will become of her.'

When I go into the garden, my elder sister shakes the flowers she has gathered at me. 'Oh … you! I have told you a hundred times not to question grown-ups. If you keep on like this, one day these people will beat you so hard you will die.' 'I will ask questions. I will. I will,' I answer crying. 'Then go and die,' says my elder sister, and continues to thread a garland for Naani's Gopalji.

Naani stands by her and says loudly, 'You are my precious Lakshmi,' with the intention that I should hear.

In the afternoons I tell the younger children horror stories of ghosts and demons who lived in the walnut tree. I tell them that if they should wake up at twelve o'clock on a full-moon night they would see children being bathed in blood. They would also hear the ghosts speaking through their noses which at first is difficult to follow. The children follow me all over the house like mice following the Pied Piper.

Bari Maami and Ma give us money to buy sweet-sour golis just to get rid of us in the afternoon. Their room has been darkened by sticking green paper on the windows, and it is full of women—Ma, Maami, Maasis and Naani. They eat all the time and have cushiony arms, fat half-naked legs and wrinkled stomachs. Then why do they keep telling us not to sit with our legs spread out? 'You all look like cows,' I tell the women, but no one seems to have heard me. Chhoti Maasi, who is lying on the floor with a pillow under her head takes a sour goli from us, starts sucking it and says, 'Jijaji is really the limit.' Suddenly laughter explodes in the room. Who? Why? How? I look all around the room for an answer, but no one is bothered about us here, they are too lost in their own conversation. I leave the room and bang hard on the door from outside, wondering if Ma will call me a nuisance. No one comes out to reprimand me, though.

'Move aside,' says Hari's mother who is carrying a tray

laden with glasses of tea into the room. 'Move. This is not for you, it's for the grown-ups. Move out of my way.' Hari's mother's nose is like a frog's and her eyebrows meet above her nose. Whenever she laughs, her cheeks hang loose like dead bats. 'Do move aside,' she says to me again. 'I won't,' I say, and try to block her way. 'I'll move only if you say girls are nice.' 'All right, all right, I have said it, so now move out of the way,' says Hari's mother. 'No,' I persist, 'say it properly.'

'Oh, Hari's ma, what's happening?' asks Maasi irritably from the room. 'Are you going to bring the tea next year, or what?' Hari's mother knits her thick eyebrows together and says. 'This Lali's middle daughter won't let me ...' She starts laughing, and as she does so her frog-like nose bobs up and down. I can hear Ma naming me and saying, 'That girl must be harassing her. She was born only to plague my life.' Someone in the room advises her that she should not get angry in her condition.

For a long time I sit outside the house watching the birds flying and wishing that I had been born a bird. 'Do mother birds too think their girl birds are inferior?' I wonder. Then I hear a voice calling, 'Where has she gone?' And I know someone is searching for me. I hide behind the wall where no one can ever find me. I wish, I wish that somewhere, anywhere, I could find that magic betel nut which would make me invisible as soon as I put it in my mouth. What wonderful fun that would be.

In the evening, when Naani finishes her story, she says, 'Now off you go to sleep, all of you.' My younger sister has already fallen asleep and Hari's mother carries her away into our room. I ask Naani if I can sleep next to her. Naani's body is soft and warm and her quilt smells of cardamom and cloves. Besides, Naani keeps a torch under her pillow. If you take it with you to the bathroom after the lights are off, you don't knock your toes against anything. But Naani says, 'No, as it is this boy doesn't

Mrinal Pande

leave me. Where is the space on this bed for the two of you? Go and sleep next to your mother. I'll tell you another story tomorrow. All right?' Naani's tone becomes sugary in the way of most grown-ups when they want to coax you into doing something. In the other room, my elder sister asks with her back turned to me, 'Did she let you sleep with her?' Her voice seems to be trembling with anger. Ma is snoring away. The clock ticks on. How can you sleep? Tick. Tick. Khrr. Khrr.

'Where are you? Girls?' calls Naani with a tray of crimson powder in her hands. In front of her there is a dish of halwa and a plate filled with puris. She has prepared those as offerings to the devi on Ashtami day. A mat has been spread in front of her for us to sit on. 'Come on girls, let me put the tikka on your foreheads.' She lights the camphor for aarti. 'Come now, let me do aarti to all of you.' My two sisters and Maama's beautiful daughters sit cross-legged in front of Naani. Naani puts a tikka on each forehead and then rings a bell. Exactly like the guard on the train. After the bell rings, she blows the conch. 'Poo-ooo.' I am suddenly transformed into a railway engine and race around the ledge of the courtyard. Inside, the room is filled with smells of camphor, halwa, ghee, and flowers. I shout, 'Come on, pay your fares to go to Calcutta. Poo-ooo.'

In the background I hear Naani saying, 'Come on dear, let me put the tikka on you. You are my kanyakumari, aren't you?'

'No,' I retort, 'I'm an engine.' Maama's son claps his hands with excitement and says, 'Oh, an engine, an engine.'

Suddenly I see Ma waddling towards me with a clenched fist and my stomach grows tight with fear. Her face is filled with rage. 'I'll make an engine out of you this very minute.'

The elderly neighbour intervenes, catches hold of Ma's hand and says, 'Have you gone mad, Lali?' She signals to me to obey, and adds, 'She is after all a child, a kanyakumari. Today is Ashtami, the devi's day; mustn't hit a kanyakumari, it is a sin.'

I jump down from the ledge with a thud and see Naani serving the other girls halwa-puri with a tightly clenched mouth.

'Go on. Take the prasad from Naani. Why do you make your mother cry when she is in this condition?' Maasi asks me irritably.

'When you people don't love girls, why do you pretend to worship them?' My voice breaks into a sob and I feel so furious with myself that I want to swallow the burning camphor to choke my treacherous throat. I want to ask 'Why' again but don't risk it because I am afraid I will start to cry. I don't want to cry in front of them.

Hari's mother puts her hand up to her cheek and says in wonder, 'Ma-ri-ma, just listen to her. What a temper for a girl to show!'

Naani is distributing a rupee and a quarter to each girl. She addresses the wall, 'You can buy twenty sour golis with this money' and holds out a twenty-five paisa coin wrapped in a rupee note towards me. I notice the mark of the crimson powder on the tip of her thumb, like a bloodstain.

I start moving back towards the wall and screaming, 'I don't want all this halwa-puri, tikka or money. I don't want to be a goddess.' I scream so loudly that the pigeons pecking at the scattered grain in the courtyard take off in a flurry, as if a bullet had been fired somewhere.

— *Translated from the Hindi by Rama Baru*

Ashapurna Devi

Izzat

'She is about fourteen or fifteen, Boudi,' is what she said, but the girl looked at least seventeen or eighteen. And how had Basanti managed to raise such a girl in that basti of theirs? Where had such health come from? And such beauty?

Sumitra could not conceal her surprise. 'She is a regular beauty. She hardly appears to be your daughter!'

Basanti smiled, a mixture of shame and pride. 'That's what they've all been saying ever since she was this little. She takes after her father, see? He was a very handsome man, died of a snakebite. And then the mother-in-law started off at me, as though I had become a snake to harm her son. That kind of hell made me come away to a free life here. Well, no one had seen that man, Boudi. So they tease and say, You must have stolen a girl from the babus!'

Sumitra smiled slightly and said, 'I feel the same, you know. You had been working for all these days, and I did not even know you had such a daughter.'

The pride on Basanti's face faded somewhat. 'I used to bring her along with me when she was little, and she helped me quite a bit. But once she was grown up, she just didn't want to leave the house at all. I'll do all your housework, was what she would say, I feel shy to go to the babu's houses … So I told her, Well, if you don't want to go, don't ... But there are dangers with such a girl, as I've just told you. If you would be kind enough to give her shelter ...'

Although Sumitra had said that Basanti had been working for her 'all these days', it really had not been that long a time. Her old servant had gone home and that was when Basanti had come to work for four months. Sumitra remembered her as she was polite and neat in her work. But that didn't warrant her coming up with such an absurd proposal as 'Keep the girl.'

There were a few goondas who had come into the basti and they had made life difficult for Basanti's daughter. The mother had her livelihood to earn and couldn't sit at home all day and guard her daughter. One had to slave the whole day to feed two people, and then there was the rent for the house. It was just a while ago that God had been kind to her and a job with a fat salary had come Basanti's way. She had to 'manage' a rich old lady. Seventy rupees as salary, with meals, oil and soap, and paan-dokta and tea besides. All she had to do was look after the old woman and run errands for her. The old woman was crippled by rheumatism, but she had elegant tastes. Basanti had to soap her during her bath, do up her hair with scented oil, rub her with powder after the oil massage for rheumatism ... how much could the daughter-in-law do? In any case, they could afford it. That's why they had gone out of their way to keep Basanti at such high wages.

'I was getting along so happily, Boudi,' said Basanti. 'I would be there by five in the morning and would get back at ten. The girl would wait at other people's homes until I got back. I never had my dinner at the babus' house. I'd bring my share home and it did fine for the two of us. We hardly spent anything. She boiled a little rice for herself in the afternoons. I'd been saving the salary for a few months for her marriage. But Boudi, the way things change ...'

Ashapurna Devi

Basanti's voice took on a philosophical note. 'That man, God, is quite a miser. He just doesn't know how to give with open hands. If he gives with one hand, he snatches away everything with the other. Happiness didn't last for very long. The old woman has started something new these days. She stays awake the whole night and makes people run errands. She'll wake up her sons and her daughters-in-law and tell them, Switch on the lights, switch on the fan. Then she'll say, Give me some water, or Make me a paan. And if you're a little late she starts cursing. Those sons work hard the whole day, running that big business. How are they to bear such demands at night? And now they're after me: We'll pay you ten rupees more, you'd better spend the nights here. If you don't agree, then we'll have to keep someone else. And here I've gone and thrown away my regular washing jobs. And now what am I to do? These rich people can get rid of you whenever they want to.'

Not knowing exactly how to respond, Sumitra said, 'Quite right.'

'But Boudi, you can't settle it by just saying, Quite right. I've come to your door, now it's all in your hands—you can kill her or keep her.'

Sumitra understood Basanti's problem and was sympathetic but she didn't understand why it should be her door, when there were doors all over the country. Basanti must have worked for so many people all these years of her life and she had only worked for Sumitra for a few months. Besides, what about the people she was working for now? What about those people who were willing to pay ten rupees more to keep Basanti during the nights to look after the invalid?

So she told Basanti, 'Why don't you take her there with you, since you say it's a huge house that these rich people have ... You can keep an eye on your daughter while you watch over the patient.'

Basanti beat her forehead and she said in an aggrieved voice, 'And have I not said as much to them. I've begged and pleaded. But the babus are very hard. The house is full of servants, they say. And since then, these last two days I've been going around to all the houses I know of, looking for shelter. No one's agreed. All of them come up with different excuses. I've been taking the girl with me. Perhaps the babus will feel kindly if they see her. But ...'

Sumitra thought to herself, 'And that's where you've made a wrong move, my Basantibala. If you hadn't shown them your daughter, somebody may have agreed.' Who would agree to keep this fire hazard in their home? Who would give her shelter? And Basanti not being there either? How would it ever work out?

The girl stood in a corner of the verandah wearing a coarsely spun striped saree. And an equally cheap-looking red blouse, probably bought off the pavements. She looked stunning even in these clothes. If you saw her once, you would want to see her again. How beautiful this girl would look if she were well-dressed and lived a life of some comfort. Sumitra decided to give her some of her old sarees and blouses and mentally sorted out the precise ones she would give. The georgette with the red flowers was a little worn out in parts, but the colour was still very bright. She'd give her that. The blue Bangalore was intact, but it was quite out of fashion now and was lying in the heap of her discarded clothes. That too, she would give. There were also a couple of printed sarees faded by repeated trips to the dhobi. And there were innumerable blouses which would fit the girl. In her mind's eye, she dressed up the girl in the red and blue sarees. She had once bought some powder manufactured by an unknown company to help out a canvassing sales girl. It was still there, unused. She decided to give that to the girl as well.

She felt pity for the girl and was sorry that such a girl was born a maidservant's daughter and had to rot away in the basti.

But some presents would assuage her uneasiness.

Basanti had said, 'It's a tiger's cave that we live in, Boudi—a snake pit. That girl's beauty spells doom.'

Sumitra was unable to discover any means of protecting her from the tiger and snake, but she was busy spinning out ways of enhancing this doomed beauty. The strange thing was, she could not detect the contradiction in her own thoughts. Her silence encouraged Basanti. 'Mounang sammati lakshanam,' as they say. Considering Sumitra's silence to be a sign of her willingness, Basanti eagerly went on, 'Then shall I leave her here from today, Boudi? She'll eat your leftovers, and will work as much as she can. If you let her enter the kitchen she'll do all your cooking. And whatever housework you tell her to …'

Sumitra became a bit absent-minded and said softly, 'It's not the work, I already have people to do the work. And there's not much cooking to be done for two people. But I'm wondering … I haven't yet asked your Dadababu …'

Basanti realized that she had softened and hastily added pressing home her advantage, 'And what is there to ask Dadababu? Whatever you are, so is Dadababu. In the home, you are queen. You don't have male servants in your house, that's why I've come to you. Please don't say No any more. I'll come back either today or tomorrow and hand her over with her clothes. Joyi, come here and take the dust off your Maima's feet. You're going to live here. You'll do everything as your Maima says, help her out in every way. Until you get married and go off to your in-laws, this house of your Maima's is going to be your home.'

Sumitra, however, hesitated a bit. 'But, I was saying, is she going to like being …'

'No more buts, Boudi,' Basanti continued in an emotional voice. 'How can she not like being here with a person such as you? What all you say! Living there in the jaws of Yama, the girl has quite shrivelled up. Those haramzada boys, whether you look or not, they'll whistle at her, sing obscene songs, make rude gestures, push past her every time she goes to the pump to fetch water. And as for the other things, it would be sinful to even talk about them.' Basanti lowered her voice and then proceeded to tell her about these 'sinful' episodes.

Sumitra was shocked.

Basanti put her anchal to her eyes and said, 'Why do you think I've been pleading with you. We're poor people who wash dishes to earn our living. But for us women, isn't there a question of izzat too? You are educated people with so much learning. You understand it all. It's up to you now to keep her izzat.'

Sumitra's heart began to beat wildly. There were tigers waiting to pounce on that beautiful girl. If she wanted to, she could save her. A hooded snake hissed over that girl's head, and if Sumitra showed a little kindness she could protect her. Wasn't she going to do even that much? Would it really be so difficult for her if a poor girl was given shelter in a corner of the house?

A frantic mother's heart wanted to entrust Sumitra with the responsibility of safeguarding the izzat of her vulnerable young girl. Was Sumitra going to ignore that? The plea was being laid at the door of her conscience and was she going to shut that door? Was she going to say, 'You take care of your daughter's izzat. Why should you try to dump your responsibility on me?' But she could not say that and said the only thing she could.

Overjoyed, Basanti began to cry. Now there was no stopping her. She could not be dissuaded from falling at Sumitra's feet. And, as she rubbed that hand on her own head and her face, she said, 'I knew you would be kind. You are Bhagawati herself. All the many houses I've been to, they just wouldn't listen to what I had to say.'

Then, she added with some embarrassment, 'So let me keep

her here for now Boudi, and go tell them at the big house. I'll fetch her at night. Tonight, mother and daughter, we'll eat together and I'll bring her over in the morning with her saree and blouse.'

Sumitra smiled and thought, 'I shall not let your daughter lack for clothes.'

Sumitra then opened her almirah and sat down to sort through her old clothes. Basanti was going to be amazed when she came next time to see her daughter. The girl was not just beautiful, there was something pleasing and respectable about the expression on her face. Sumitra was going to give her a new life. She was going to teach her to read and write. Sumitra began to think on those lines, unmindful of her own position.

But Mohitosh was quite aware of Sumitra's position. So he cried out in violent objection, 'What do you mean you've given her your word? You didn't even think it was necessary to ask me once?'

'She begged me ...' Sumitra replied in some confusion.

'And why wouldn't she? They're ready to lick the dust off your feet if it means getting the job done. That doesn't mean that you have to take on such a responsibility. Impossible!'

'The girl can't survive at their basti anymore.' said Sumitra with some force. 'She can't because she is a good, respectable girl. If she was bad, she would've been ruined a long time ago in that environment. Are we to throw a girl like this to the wolves?'

'There are all sorts of things happening in the world,' said Mohitosh. 'Are you capable of being responsible for everyone?'

'If not for everyone, at least for one person.'

'Forget those poetic sentiments!' retorted Mohitosh, heatedly. 'You must act after the proper consideration. I've seen the girl. A girl like that can't remain good in such low-class surroundings.'

Sumitra replied, her face bright red, 'Whatever they may be, there is no reason for you to talk like a lower-class person. If that is indeed the case, then why should her mother come to me, so upset and so anxious?'

'They are up to all kinds of tricks.'

'What sort of trick can you be thinking of?' asked Sumitra in a low voice. 'If you had heard everything you wouldn't have been able to say No either. Some scoundrels have started plaguing her so much that she's told her mother, One day Ma, you'll come back home to find me hanging from the beam.'

'But why does the mother need to take up that job?'

'Look, we all need money. They need it even more. The poor thing has been thinking about her daughter's marriage.'

Mohitosh said scornfully, 'How many thousands do you need for a maidservant's daughter's wedding?'

Sumitra was hurt and could not bear his contempt for the poor. Her voice hardened. 'Let's forget all that for a minute. Do you think that even if she sits there guarding her daughter, she will be able to do so? She's quite helpless. They'll probably snatch her away before her very eyes.'

But Mohitosh retorted sarcastically, 'I see they've come up with a lot of stories to win over their Boudi. Don't talk to me about them—they can really cook up stories. She's made up this rigmarole to foist her daughter on you! What are you going to do if she now calls the police and tells them that the babus have forcibly taken away her daughter?'

Sumitra was obliged to sit down. 'I find that they are not the only ones capable of cooking up stories. How did you even think of such a thing?'

'Why shouldn't I? I don't go around looking at the wold through rose-tinted glasses like you do! Do you know about the kind of scams that go on in a place like Calcutta? Are you aware at all how regularly these kind of cases come up? You'll find that that very same girl will strip off your mask of respectability and say, Yes, the babus had brought me along to work for them, and now they won't let me go ... If they want, they can even trump up a scandalous charge against me.'

'And what is she to get out of it?' Sumitra's voice was as hard as stone.

'Anyone would think that you've just been born. Don't you know what she's going to get out of it? Squeeze money out of us. Those goondas she mentioned, quite possibly they're her accomplices. They'll come over to our house to gherao and abuse us. It's unthinkable. Get rid of her right away. You said something about her coming over at night. Well, you can tell her then, it's not going to work. Dadababu hasn't agreed.'

Sumitra looked at him steadily. 'This means I have to tell this maidservant that I have no say in this household.'

Mohitosh said with utter disregard for her words, 'And what a person before whom your prestige is going to be shattered! Keep your poetry aside and try to be a little practical. Supposing that all I've told you actually happens, what will you do then?'

'And supposing nothing of that sort happens. Supposing that by some strange chance that maidservant is actually telling the truth?'

'Well, she should sort out her own daughter's problems. Why can't she talk to all the people in the basti?'

'Then you think that if she were to tell all the people in the basti they would take the responsibility of protecting her izzat?'

Mohitosh replied with some enthusiasm, 'And why shouldn't they? Not everyone is a bad sort. A lot of respectable types live there with their families. If they all come together it won't take long to silence those goondas.'

'Then you believe that those basti people have more humanity than you? And more power?'

'Go on, say what you like,' said Mohitosh. 'But I'm not

going to agree to let your Basantibala's daughter stay here. Even if we assume it is not a trap, that girl herself is quite capable of causing a scandal in our home.'

A faint and somewhat twisted smile played around Sumitra's lips. 'With whom? We have no male servants in the house.'

Mohitosh laughed heartily. 'Well, perhaps with the master. With her kind of stunning looks!'

Sumitra said in a low voice, 'That's all the more reason, isn't it, why we should in fact keep her? To find out what is brass and what is gold.'

'Stop talking nonsense!' he retorted angrily. 'When her mother comes you had better tell her that there's no question of shelter here.'

'You can do the telling.'

'I? Why should it be me? I don't talk to these maidservant types of yours. You will tell her whatever has to be said.'

'I can't. I've given her my word.'

'If you go around giving your word without considering your position, you are bound to be in an uncomfortable situation,' said Mohitosh angrily. 'A maidservant comes, tells you a load of rubbish, and gets you to make her some kind of a promise, and now so much talk of being bound by it! All right, if you can't tell her, I shall.'

And so he did.

Sumitra could hear them from her room. She heard Basanti's tearful voice pleading, 'Dadababu, please call Boudi, just once. We had agreed and I went to tell the people in the big house ...'

Mohitosh's voice was hard. 'Boudi has a headache. She's lying down.'

'Let me go to the door then, Dadababu. I'll tell her, Boudi, don't dash my hopes ...'

'No! No! She mustn't be disturbed. She's very unwell and can't even lift her head.'

Basanti cried some more and at that moment Sumitra heard a voice filled with anguish. 'That's enough, Ma. Come away. There's no need to cry out and call on Boudi. It's clear who has the last word in this house. You're not to fall at their feet, thinking of your daughter's izzat. The babus don't care about the izzat of a low-class girl. All right. If we are low-down people, we'll have to settle for a low-down life. If we have to go to the dogs then that's what we'll do.'

Sumitra heard two pairs of feet pounding down the stairs and then ... silence.

Mohitosh entered the room and demanded, 'Did you hear them talk? And that's the girl you thought was civilized. Respectable! Huh!'

Sumitra could not reply. She truly could not lift her head. It felt as if it was being torn apart because she did not have the power to look after a young woman's izzat.

But which young woman's?

—*Translated from the Bangla by Rimli Bhattacharya*

Amrita Pritam

Kanjak

The darkness of night had not yet melted into dawn when Daropati arose from her string-bed with a start. She awakened thus everyday, very early in the morning. Today was her seventh fast of the nauratra week.

Pouring kerosene oil on the twigs in the hearth, Daropati lit a fire and put a few potatoes in the kettle to boil. Before beginning the day-long fast, she would make a meal of mashed potatoes sweetened with sugar. During this period of fasting she, like other devotees, was forbidden to eat salt or wheat.

The following morning, she thought she would rise even earlier. That being the day of Ashtami feasting, she had to feed kanjaks, young unmarried girls who are feted on such occasions. She would cook puris to be eaten with gram and potatoes, seasoned in ghee and spices. She would prepare halwa, light the candles and invite kanjaks from all the families in the neighbourhood. She would wash their feet, apply sindoor to their foreheads and tie the sacred thread round their wrists. Then she would lay out the trays of food before them with two pice apiece as an offering.

Daropati recalled how a long time ago, when she was just about nine years, she was given by her mother a pink dupatta to wear. Light green glass-bangles dangling on her arms, she had gone to her aunt's house as a kanjak on Ashtami day. This aunt was her mother's friend, and they were bound to each other in sisterly affection by a mutual vow.

Daropati was a kanjak, a maiden of barely ten, when she was betrothed to one of the aunt's nephews, then eleven or twelve. A few months later they were married.

But, as the custom was, Daropati returned home after a day's stay at her parents-in-law's home. She was not to go back until two years later. But she was no longer a kanjak, she was a wife.

There were still fifteen months left of those two years when her young husband was taken ill and died. There was mourning in the family. Daropati was no longer a wife, but a widow.

She had not seen her husband at the time of the wedding, nor after that. The only time she had seen him was when she had gone to her aunt's house as one of the kanjaks on Ashtami day.

Tomorrow Daropati would feed kanjaks. She would wash their tiny feet with her hands. She would tie the red-and-white thread round their small, delicate wrists, and then she would bow to them in obeisance. Those little goddesses—she herself was now upwards of three score years—those kanjak-maidens. … Her forehead lowered as she ruminated. Her eyes on the ground, she saw her own feet—long, chapped and wrinkled. She started. Kanjak-maidens, she thought, had small, white feet and thin, rounded wrists. She looked at her own arms: there were no glass-bangles on those masses of limp, feeble flesh.

'Amman,' broke in a voice from the room adjacent to the kitchen. Daropati suddenly remembered that she had put potatoes in the kettle to boil and that she had yet to prepare tea for Malti.

'Coming, daughter,' she answered, as she replaced the kettle on the fire.

Of course, Malti was not her daughter. She ⸺ ⸺ ⸺ ghter of her husband's younger brother.

Two years after her wedding, Daropati was to be escorted to her parents-in-law's home by her husband. But he died, with a year and three months to go for that day. For the honour of his name, the young widow had been brought into his parents' house. Here she had lived for five patient decades.

In time, Daropati lost her father-in-law and mother-in-law, and her own parents. She had a brother-in-law, the younger brother of her deceased husband, and his wife, and she continued to live in the house with them.

Her sister-in-law did not have a son and both of them were sad about it. 'Who will throw sweets over our biers,' they often rued, 'if there is no male heir in the family? Who will offer water to the souls of our ancestors at the time of the annual feasting?'

Then after some time the sister-in-law gave birth to a son. There was another after two years, then another. Daropati became absorbed in bringing up her sister-in-law's children, and was reassured that there would now be a male member in the family to perform the last rites for her when she died.

All the children called her Amman. Her brother-in-law also called her Amman instead of Bhabi. The distinction between the two terms was hardly of any significance to her.

*

The kettle started to simmer and hiss. Daropati hurriedly lumped tea-leaf into the pot and poured the hot water over it. She picked up the cup and saucer with the utmost care and, laying out milk, sugar and the tea-pot on the tray, went into Malti's room. Quietly she put the tray on the small table by the bed. She was almost afraid to touch these China articles. They were so delicate and required such care in handling. All her life Daropati had drunk her lassi from a bronze bowl and her tea from a brass vessel. Since the children who called her Amman had grown up and started going to college, they had ceased drinking their tea from the tall metal jars. They had brought from the market cups and saucers and taught their aunt how to use them and how to brew tea without boiling it over the fire. So long as the children had listened to her, she gave them milk with plenty of cream on top of it. Now they drank thin black tea, telling her that buffalo's heavy milk encumbered the brain.

*

Since yesterday that young man to whom Malti was to be married had been staying in the house. He was sleeping in the next room, and Malti asked Amman to give him tea also.

As Daropati stepped inside the room, the young man who was fast asleep turned on his side. From the folds of the rug under which he had curled himself cosily, a few fragments of broken glass fell noisily to the floor. Daropati stood dazed, as those bits of glass shimmered before her dim eyes, describing an interminable chain of tremulous, bangle-like circles. She felt a choking in her throat and her feet trembled as she walked out of the room.

As if to deflect her mind, Malti, who had heard the glass pieces fall on the floor, said, 'Is not it today, Amman, that you must fasten the thread round our wrists and feed us halwa and puri?'

'No, daughter! Not today. That will be tomorrow.'

Daropati could say no more and came back to the kitchen.

She would seat the kanjaks in a row the following morning, kanjak-maidens, big and small. Malti would also be one of them, and she, old woman of three score and more, would bow before them and do them homage! A wrinkle appeared on Daropati's brow in the midst of her meditations. There would be kanjak-maidens of ten, twelve, fifteen coming to the house tomorrow. She herself was a kanjak-maiden of more than sixty. Would she bow to them all, including Malti? Her forehead stiffened.

For the sake of her deceased husband she had observed nauratra fasts religiously for half a century. She had fed hundreds of kanjaks. Many of these kanjak-maidens would be married women by the time nauratras came round the following year and their places would be taken by new ones. She remembered having fed and worshipped the daughters of those who had themselves come to their house as kanjaks. Kanjaks came and went like water buckets in the well, but none of them remained a kanjak all her life.

Today she felt as if the earth had split into two; as if the lifelong bond had finally burst. Her heart wrung in pain. She felt a sensation of revulsion rise in her. A giddiness overtook her and her hands trembled. Then, tightening her lips, she rose and threw into the sink the potatoes she had been kneading with groundnut powder for the morning's meal before beginning the seventh nauratra fast. She picked up a handful of forbidden wheat grain from the earthen jar in the far corner of the kitchen and thrust it into her toothless mouth.

The first rays of the sun discovered Daropati lying on the floor of the kitchen, unconscious.

—*Translated from the Punjabi by Harbans Singh*

Amrita Pritam

Baburao Bagul

Death Comes Cheap

My friend, the Poet, and I were at home. He sprawled on the bed and pulled out the papers which were in his pocket. 'I'm going to set into verse the stuff I wrote earlier,' he said. 'Meanwhile, you work at your story, develop it further ...' I set to work on the story, tried to take it forward, but the story would not move ahead. Just as I tore the paper to bits, my friend said, 'This poem refuses to take shape. I'll read out the rough draft to you—

'This is Mumbai ...

... Mumbai was the first city to dream of freedom. And the first to actually witness freedom ...

... The age of technology was born in Mumbai. And the light of the industrial revolution first shone on the streets of Mumbai and then spread out in all directions ... This is a huge city. An enlightened city. And it is an epic poem. The streets of Mumbai are the verses of this poem.

... The idea of freedom came to a flood in Mumbai. And the pure waters of freedom flowed down the streets of Mumbai into every village of this country. Because these streets are bathed with the blood of martyrs. And this city is horrifyingly awesome, like Shiv ...'

'Well, what do you think? I'm going to cut and polish these

gems and set them in verse and give Marathi poetry a valuable jewel.'

I stretched my legs out on the table and said, 'Give.' And picking up my story I wrote the title, 'Death Comes Cheap in Mumbai'.

'What did you write?'

'Death Comes Cheap in Mumbai.'

'Great. Now you will be able to get the story going.' And he started working on his poem. But the poem refused to flow. He rubbed out every sentence that he wrote, wrote another and when the page was full, he tore it up and started on a fresh one. And I was fed up too, fed up of filling pages with unsatisfactory words. Frustrated, I finally gave up. 'Let's go for a walk,' I said.

'This damn poem refuses to fit into its mould. I have been twisting it round but it still won't fit in. It's as stubborn as a rock. Let's go ...'

We both came out on the street and started walking down the main road. There were rail tracks along the road and on one side of the tracks were many huts, one below the other. On the other side were shops, a bank and a school. Someone called out to me from one of the huts, 'Teacher ...'

I turned to look. Bhimu Kadam staggered up to me. 'It's smooth as brandy. Will you have some? I was drinking and I saw you, so I called out. Come.'

'I've eaten already, so I won't have any now. But who brought it? You or the woman?'

'That damn woman has disappeared again since yesterday. I don't think she is going to come back soon. I thrashed her because she was always suspicious of the Madrasi woman next door. Earlier she suspected the black bead seller. And before that she was suspicious of that young girl, the one who is now decaying and dying. Teacher, that damn girl must be just about sixteen or seventeen years old now, but she is rotting from inside and outside. She is just a bag of bones but still swings her backside when she walks. She started too early. Her mother was like that, too—left her young daughter and ran off with a strange man. And to tell you the truth, teacher, I don't like women. What do they have? Skin and bones ...

'Didn't I commit murder for a woman and ruin my life? Since then I am fed up of women and wine, they make me angry. When I have money I head for the bottle. Otherwise there is the packet of ganja. And if she starts fighting, starts crying and begging, or gets suspicious of other women then I go to her. I am fed up. Well, I'll be going. Look, look that scarecrow is staring at you. I'm going. Some damn person will come and finish my drink.'

He went off to his hut to finish his drink. And we looked at the girl who was staring at us. She was standing by the old sacks and rags which made up her shack. Her face was swollen and there were black and brown spots on it; her sari was just a rag. And there was no way of telling whether she had eaten or was hungry. But she looked tired and emaciated.

'What a horrible lesson life has taught this child of seventeen. Her mother abandoned her and so she had to take up prostitution to feed herself. It is like a damn birthmark. But who gave it to her? And why ... Come, let's go ...'

We looked at the huts as we walked ahead. The railway fencing supported them. Each hut was about four or five feet tall along the fencing and skimmed the ground on the other side along the road. The old sacks and jute rags were weighed down with stones to prevent them from flying away. My friend looked at the huts and at Bhimu drinking straight from the bottle in his hut. 'He seems very defeated, hopeless. As if he only wishes to die. Do you know anything about him?'

'Yes, I do. His name is Bhimu Kadam and he comes from the Satara region. He belongs to a Maratha Kshatriya family.

Once there was inherited wealth in the family, which one of his ancestors frittered away completely. After that, Bhimu was the only one who had earned himself some kind of name and fame. But then he committed a murder.'

'Who did he kill?'

'His wife.'

'Why?'

'I'll tell you. At that time he was a wrestler. His fame had spread to all the villages around. Villagers trembled at the sight of him and everybody respected him. In this way, he was regaining the respect that his family had lost. His fame grew and the means to this fame was his body. He refused to have any physical relations with his wife, just so that his fame would grow. But in the same village lived a man whose family, for many generations, had enmity with Bhimu's family. This man started seducing his wife. Deprived of all physical relations, his wife succumbed within months. She did whatever he asked of her. Naturally, this gossip spread like fire through the village and the flames soon singed Bhimu.

'One day, instead of going to the akhada, he returned home and found his enemy and his wife together. He killed them with his axe. Then he went straight to the police station and gave himself up.

'When he was released from jail, he had become depressed and cynical and did not return to the village. He did not even look for a regular job. Instead, he did all kinds of odd jobs, whatever came his way. He spent some money on food and the rest on alcohol and slept wherever he found place to lie down. He spent five years like this, floating around like garbage on the streets. Then he met this woman in the slums along the coast in Bandra. She is a sweeper from Kutch. If you see her you will be amazed—she is voluptuous, fair and has kajal-lined eyes. She cleans the toilets in some houses in a few buildings.

She even supplies illicit liquor to some people in the houses where she works. She's very coquettish, and cunning. After five years of drifting around alone, Bhimu felt the need for a wife. So he started living with her. She liked him so much that she worked and earned and supported him. She bore his bouts of intense depression and the beatings he gave her. On the insistence of a friend, Bhimu took up a job at the slaughterhouse killing sheep and goats. Depression and dejection with life had changed him so much that he did not mind such a job and in just a few days he became skilled in skinning the carcasses. But one day, when he was running his knife through the neck of a goat, he happened to glance at its eye. In it he saw the same expression that had been in his wife's eyes when he had killed her. Her struggles against him were echoed in the throes of the dying goat. And sharp as the edge of a sword came to him the confession he had made in court, "Saheb, my family name had been mired in disgrace for many generations. I had begun to lift it out, to bring some glory to it again. And if my wife had just waited a little longer, had a little patience, she would not have died. But she began to demolish the dignity of my family, and ruin my penance. She challenged my manhood. And so I responded and used the axe on her and her man. I have no desire to live any more. Please hang me …"'

'Is that what he said? Wonderful! Then what happened?'

'He remembered this, and was so filled with vengeance that he went wild and chopped into the frightened, bleating sheep and goats with his knife until the other workers rushed to him and took the knife away from him. He not only lost his job but also had to pay for all the mutton he had ruined and the damage he had caused. Then he went into such intense depression that he wouldn't even eat, wouldn't sleep. He just sat in one place as if he was deaf and dumb. Or he would yell and shout and go berserk. Then there was a flood and all the huts along the Bandra coast were swept away. He collected whatever stuff he could save from the flood and built another hut at a new place. The municipality workers came along and demolished it. He took what remained and came here. When this breaks, he will probably build another. Or maybe, he won't even bother to build another. Someday, just as casually as he has ganja, or a drink, he will walk on to the tracks and die.'

'And his wife—I mean that sweeper—will find another man,' my poet friend said.

'She has found many others already. She is often away for a week. He never says a word. Not because he's henpecked or because he is dependent on her, but because he is as sad and detached as a sadhu. Life is a penance for him. His heart has died. Or maybe his sorrow is something different ...'

'What a horrific character! You should write a story on him. Call it "Death is as Cheap as Mud".'

A train clattered past. We both looked at it. In its light we saw four or five women squatting by the tracks with mugs of water beside them. Embarrassed, we lowered our eyes. With his head bent, my friend, the Poet asked, 'Whose hut is that?'

'That belongs to Ranu Nagvekar. He suffers from TB. He has four kids. His wife does housework in some of the flats around here and he polishes shoes. But the young shoeshine boys don't let him work. If he does get a client and he coughs, the client covers his nose and mouth with a cloth to avoid the TB germs and goes away. Some pay him for half the work; others don't pay him at all. It is because of him that I have become familiar with this slum. I was walking in the park one evening when there was a lot of shouting. I saw people running towards a man who was writhing on the ground. I joined them. I saw Ranu Nagvekar pressing his chest and moaning and writhing in pain. He was soaked with sweat. When I asked around, I came to know that his wife was ill, he had four kids and suffered from TB. To earn at least a few paise he would grab the shoes of passers-by. Or if someone had taken off his chappals, he would start polishing them. So he had grabbed at the feet of that man and tried to take off his shoe. The man shook his leg hard to free it and inadvertently kicked Ranu in the chest. So here was Ranu in intense pain. A young man in loud clothes, who looked like a vagabond, was rubbing his chest. Another old man, belonging to the middle class, was fanning him with the scarf he wore round his shoulders. And many men had surrounded the young ass who had kicked Ranu. Some said that he should be taken to the police station; a doctor should be called; he should not be allowed to go. Some even decided to beat him up. But others, more sensible, prevented this. The young man was shouting and telling them all, "He is not hurt. He is only pretending. He wants to make money."

'But Ranu's agony seemed to be growing. He began to spit bits of red sputum. The crowd saw this and turned upon the young man. He was frightened and gave Ranu a ten-rupee note. And after much pleading and begging he managed to get away.

'Later, when I met Ranu in the park, I sympathetically asked him what had happened and he told me that when the young man had said "He is doing it for money", Ranu had taken his words to heart and decided to extract money from him. "I pretended to be in greater pain than I was. I got some money and got medicines for my wife. And for a week my kids ate rice. I hold people's feet everyday so that someone should kick out at least once. But nobody kicks me. Nobody gives me ten rupees. And the shoeshine boys don't let me work. They grab the clients just like a crow picks up worms. They cheat me, tease me, make me cry. I have become a game for the little devils. Just like a flock of crows peck at an old, dying animal, these kids peck at me. They make me wish I were dead."

'Ranu was a printer in a sari printing shop. He used to

somehow manage to run his house on his meagre salary. His mother died and left him a mountain of debt to add to the ones he had incurred himself. He worked so hard to repay that debt that he became weak and contracted TB. Since he could not work well he was thrown out of his job. Nobody else would employ him. He took a large amount of deposit (pagdi) and rented out his one-room house so that he would have money to feed his family, and moved to a hut. But there were illegal brewers in that slum and they caused a fire that burned down his hut. After that he rebuilt his hut several times but each time it was demolished by the municipality. Finally, he came here. I once asked him, "Where will you stay during the monsoon?" "If I have money by the time the rains come, I will stay here, otherwise I will stay on the railway platform. Or in the shelter of the new buildings which are being constructed. What are we but people discarded by society, we must live like stray cats and dogs, anywhere …" '

'These are all people dead at heart. Their own sorrows are so overpowering that they have no place for any other thought. Suppose somebody educates them …,' said my friend, the Poet.

'Then they will set Rome on fire!'

'Come on, Kaka is calling us.' We walked past some huts.

'Aiye Janab!' We stopped beside Chacha. My friend stared in surprise at the man. Chacha had the aristocratic looks of a nawab. The Poet asked, 'Do you belong to a royal family?'

'Why?'

'How is it that you have this long straight nose? All my aristocratic Muslim friends have a nose just like this.'

'How did you hurt your head? Why is your face and head swollen?' I asked Chacha.

'I am so unlucky. Last night I went to the railway tracks to relieve myself and tripped over a rail and fell. God knows how long I lay there, unconscious. I lost a lot of blood. Then this

Ramu bhaiyya with whom I play cards came along to relieve himself. He thought he would check if there was a wallet or any valuables in the pocket of this man, so he came near. He recognized me and brought me here.'

'How are you now?'

'Look at these.' He showed us his bandaged legs.

'Where's Jalal?'

'He's gone to the station to get water.'

'Okay. See you tomorrow.' I was in a hurry to leave because Chacha always asked for money.

'Do you have fifty paise? I couldn't go to the market today.'

I gave him fifty paise and left.

'Who is he?'

'I got to know him because of the Slum Association. Chacha was once a teacher at the Hyderabad Sansthan. He knows Urdu and Farsi, and enough English to write an application. When his wife died, he gave out his fields for share-cropping and came to Mumbai, because his sons were here. His three sons had all gone the wrong way. One of them lived a completely decadent life with a woman who was a dancer, singer and prostitute. As long as he had money, she was his beloved. The moment his money was over, he became her servant. The second son was an alcoholic. And the third had two wives and more children than he could feed. His first wife died and the second one died in labour. The old man was left with all the children on his hands. A few months later, the son abandoned the children and his father and disappeared. The old man had to feed those little devils and so he sold his room and came to live on the street. He found jobs in restaurants and houses for the older kids, where they were given food for their work. Even then, he was left with two small kids. He started out in Bhendi Bazaar and with the municipal demolition squad at his heels, he lived on various streets before he came here. Seven or eight years went by while he found his way here. By this time, the elder child had left him. Now the younger child is here and begs for food for both of them. And the old man eats and chats. Once in a way he goes to the market and if someone asks him to write their accounts he does so. But he cannot see properly and does not have the means to buy himself glasses. He takes four or eight annas from people like me to buy himself a bidi. And crosses each mountainous day with the name of Allah on his lips.'

'Write a story about Chacha—"Death has Become Very Cheap". If the daughter-in-law dies it is because she has been killed by too many pregnancies. Ten children. And their father does not care whether they live or die. He abandons them. And the old man does almost the same thing. He keeps only one of the ten children with him. At least somebody will notice the little children on the streets all the way from the Gateway to here. You must write …'

'… Look at her. The woman in the satin skirt, green blouse and transparent red odhni—she looks very alive. Of all the people we have seen so far, she is the only one who looks robust. Although she is so dark, she is very attractive.' My friend, the Poet, stared at the woman selling kerwa beads. She looked as firm as a statue carved from black stone. 'She sets out with a trunk every morning and by evening she returns with a carefully chosen man. In the trunk she has toothpastes, kumkum, wax, needles, black beads, glass beads, bracelets for small children, bindis, kerwa beads—and soaps that get rid of unwanted hair. She does some prostitution; gets a meal from the man who takes her to a hotel. In the morning, she wakes up, washes up and goes to the restaurant for breakfast.'

'… And this one hasn't even built himself a hut. Who is he?'

'Barku is from around my village, somewhere nearby. Both his legs are maimed. That is why he always sits in that sort of wheelchair. He eats in the chair and like a bull, shits there as

Baburao Bagul

well. And like a traditional Indian woman, his wife, Sarja, looks after him like a baby. The villagers call her satpativrata, a faithful and devoted wife, someone to be respected and revered. And she too refers to herself as satpativrata. Her head is filled with stories of the devoted wives of mythology; otherwise she would never have lived with Barku. Because, though Barku is disabled, he is a terror. Earlier he used to be a water carrier and also used to dig wells. He is a water diviner, he can see the water within the earth. Once when he was digging a well, the water suddenly gushed up and he crashed into the well and lost the use of his legs. He was bedridden. Like an animal he would defecate where he sat. His elder brother and sister-in-law found his filthy ways unbearable and they threw him out of the house. Barku came to Mumbai with his wife and two children. And he turned his wife and children, especially the good-looking elder daughter, into his investment, and started making money.

'When he first came to Mumbai, his mind was filled with all the thoughts of revenge and jealousy that a farmer's mind would have. He wanted to destroy those who had thrown him out of his house. He wanted to buy another field, build himself a house. He only wished to order his children to work hard in his fields. He wanted to be a richer man than his brother and more influential in the village. So he behaved just as such a man would.

'When they first came to Mumbai, the whole family lived together for eight months. They managed to save 200 to 250 rupees during that time. And since there was still the decency of a small farmer in him, he took the family back to the village during the monsoon. He deposited his money with a rich shopkeeper in the village with many people as witness, and when the monsoon was nearing an end, he returned to Mumbai. This time he observed and listened to other beggar families and decided that the family would split up and beg at different places.

It was greed for money that made him send his wife and children to different places. His wife sat with the youngest child in her lap at the entrance to the railway station. She put jaggery on her eyes to appear blind. His son was dressed as a poor brahmin boy with a sacred thread, tuft of hair on the crown of his head and kumkum on his forehead. He sat at the entrance to a temple. He got more money, fruits and sweets than the other children there. And his growing young daughter, under his instructions, washed her face clean, wore her sari tightly round her maturing body and pushed his wheelchair down the streets. She smiled back at the men who stared at her body and her face and begged for alms with folded hands. She had no problems making gestures towards young men, because she had seen her parents' nightly activities since coming to Mumbai and the desire to do the same coursed through her blood. In a few days, that is what she started doing—renting out her young body. She gave the money she earned to her father.

'His jealousy and revenge had taken such a hold of him, that he never realized how debased his family had become. He pounced on money like a hungry tiger. He just didn't care about his family. One day, his daughter handed him thirty rupees, not a small sum, and went off with a man and did not return for a month.

'When she came back, she had changed completely. She looked like a newly married young girl from a decent family. Her skin had become fair and her hair shone black. Her face bloomed like a flower. She had kumkum on her forehead and wore an expensive sari and blouse. Barku and his wife were very happy to see their daughter looking like a young brahmin girl. He indicated to her to come near him and kissed her forehead. And Sarja was pleased that even if her daughter was not married, at least she had good food to eat and a place to live, clothes to wear. It was better than her life being ruined on the streets of Mumbai. Although she was a little sad, she asked her, "Whose sari is it?"

"Hers!"

"Have you come to visit us?"

"No, he has thrown me out."

"Why?" asked Sarja, fearfully.

"His wife had gone off to her parents house in a huff. When she didn't return for three months, he took me home. She came to know of this and came with her brothers. He threw me out of the house. I came here."

'When he heard this, Barku was happy and Sarja was sad. Four times the girl gave her father money and went off to live with a man for two weeks or a month. But she did not get the comforts that she had got the first time. One of them even tried to sell her off on Foras Road. After that she was afraid to go off with complete strangers, and preferred to work right there. But she asked each of the men who took her for a few minutes, "Will you take me away from here? Will you rent a room and marry me?" But none of them wanted to marry her. At most they would take her to Haji Malang or a similar convenient place. She got fed up of sleeping in the dust of the footpath, of living on the streets and giving her body to any vagabond for whatever little money he offered. The way her parents and she herself slept with any man on the streets in the open like animals began to disgust her. She had neither respect nor love for her parents, nor fear of them. Ever since her father had brushed away her request to build a hut, she wanted only to run away from them. Her younger brother also felt the same disgust for his parents. The filth sticking to their father's bottom, his dirty odour had become unbearable for him. Like many other children, he also wanted to go far away from his father. But like his sister, he, too, was unable to find a way out.

'They were both in this frame of mind when the monsoon

71

arrived. Barku went off to the village with only his son and his money belt loaded with cash. He left his daughter behind so that she could earn money even in the rain, and for the first time in his life he left his wife behind to ensure that she did not blow up the money or run away. If he had taken the girl with him to the village, she might have been placated. But now she knew that because of his immense greed for money he had left her behind, and she looked even more desperately for an opportunity to escape. The rains came. Sleeping in the corners or alcoves of restaurants and shops curled up like little animals while the rain poured down, or sitting up shivering through the dark cold nights when there was not a corner empty to curl up in—all this became unbearable. For one month in her young life she had experienced comfort and happiness and its memory was like a weight that pressed down cruelly on her mind and heart. So even if she was offered any amount of money, she first wanted to know where that man would take her. Earlier, any place—toilets, spaces behind huts—would be good enough. But now no amount of money could lure her there. She missed the days when in the monsoon, while the rain fell, she had a bed and a soft mattress to lie on, when she was sexually fulfilled, she had good food cooked in plenty of oil to eat, and she missed the man who had treated her gently and lovingly as if she was his lawfully wedded wife. Finally, these memories made her so deeply unhappy that she sold herself for fifty rupees, which she gave her mother, and went off with a man to a whorehouse. It was as if she fell into such a deep pit, that she never surfaced again.

'After two months Barku came back with the ownership papers of land worth 2500 rupees. Now all he needed to do was buy two bullocks and a cart and build a tiny house. When he reached Mumbai and heard that his daughter had run away, he wrote to tell his brother that his daughter had died under the wheels of a car and that he should not come to Mumbai. Instead, he himself would return soon to the village.

'Now he put the whole burden of earning for the family on his son. Every morning and evening he made him beg before the temple dressed as a brahmin boy. In the afternoons he made him polish shoes. But the boy soon stopped listening to his father and only worked as a shoeshine boy. Slowly, as he grew up, he began to distance himself from his father. Sometimes he would stay with him, sometimes he never came back even at night. In a few years he finally simply disappeared.

'Though he lost both his children his greed for money did not die. He now focussed his attention on the small boy who was just growing out of babyhood. He realized that if the child's arms and legs were deformed, he would evoke greater pity and earn more money. So he asked his wife to twist the fair, healthy child's arms and legs so that they would be deformed. She refused to do so, and so they fought all the time. Some time passed like this until one day, crying bitterly, she told him that the child had been kidnapped. After that, she would cry all the time and could hardly eat. She started insisting that they should leave Mumbai and go back to their village. But he would have none of it. She was now afraid that one day he would sell her as well.

'Ever since he had come to Mumbai and lived life on the footpaths of the city, he had lost so much, but he had no regrets about it. Because he was sure that his shoeshine boy would come back to him sooner or later. He believed that he would have many more children. Besides, somebody had given him their daughter, he had subjugated his brother, and all his in-laws respected him.

'A few more summers passed by. His hair began to grey and his body often trembled. During this time, he had three children. Like his eldest child, his fourth daughter began to mature and people noticed her. Just to earn some name and respect he arranged a large and showy engagement. But though he knew that she was in constant danger of molestation or even of losing her life, he never sent her to his village. Because her beauty earned him more money. And a horrible thing happened to this young, pretty girl. Eight or ten tough men surrounded them to snatch the girl away, and ...'

I was going to narrate the incident when the hut near us burst open and collapsed as if a bomb had gone off inside. Somebody screamed and wailed for life. We turned towards it and saw this young woman, dark as a snake, slim and firm, completely naked, run for her life from the hut. Behind her were two youths with knives. They slashed at her nude body. One of them caught her Madrasi style knot of hair and pulled her back. She screamed in terror and many men came running from the other huts. Bhimu was right in front with the empty bottle in his hands. When they saw the mob rushing towards them, the rapists jumped on to the railway tracks and began to throw the pebbles from the tracks on the crowd. Soon they disappeared into the darkness. The crowd collected round the collapsed hut.

The girl was lying on the road, blood flowing from her wounds. Somebody covered her with a rag and lifted the hut up and went inside. Within lay her husband moaning in a pool of blood. He had three or four long slashes on his body. A woman lying beside her husband had been raped right in front of his eyes. All this had shaken my friend, the Poet, to the depths of his being. In an anguished voice he said, 'Let's go.'

We walked ahead and were near the station. There was a huge crowd on the platform round the water taps. A railway policeman was encouraging the crowd along with a couple of rowdy boys in the hope that he would find some young girl there. Chacha's grandson, Jalal, with his zinc vessel, was trying to get through the crowd like a cat.

My friend said, 'I'm going to throw away whatever I wrote. I'll keep just one line—"This is Mumbai. Man eats man here. And death comes cheap …" '

—*Translated from the Marathi by Sandhya Pandey*

J. Bhagyalakshmi

The Swing

Pankajakshi stood on the balcony watching intently as her grandchildren, Sudhir, five, and Supriya, seven, played in the park across the road. She enjoyed sitting on the balcony in the mornings and evenings, watching the human drama that unfolded before her eyes. Children jumped and ran around, while older people walked around the park or exercised in the open air or relaxed on benches on the green lawn. Since she had no friends here, this is how Pankajakshi spent her time.

Supriya was standing upright on the swing. A little girl but swinging so high, thought Pankajakshi in alarm. It looked like she was concentrating all her energy on the swing. The other children around her were protesting noisily: 'Come on Supriya, that's enough. How long are you going to be on the swing? See, I have to have my turn, and then my little brother will get on.' A hundred voices were speaking at the same time, creating a loud babble. And that's when it happened. Supriya, who had been swinging really high, suddenly jumped off the swing. All the children screamed. Pankajakshi's heart missed a beat. She almost tumbled down the stairs as she rushed to her granddaughter's side. She parted the crowd of children and reached out to help Supriya up. But the girl was already on her feet, smiling and dusting the sand off her dress. She was engrossed in conversation with her friends. Pankajakshi dragged her out of the circle.

'Priya, have you hurt yourself? Why did you jump from such a height? Are you crazy?' Pankajakshi chided.

'It's all right, Ammama. I do it everyday. Only the people who are watching me get scared, I don't,' the girl laughed. 'See I'm perfectly all right. There's not even a scratch. The trick is to point your legs downwards—like this—before jumping,' she explained, as she demonstrated the action with a little leap.

'Oh, you and your games! No fear, no discipline. This is all because of the way your mother brings you up. She spoils both of you with her pampering.'

'Oh Ammama, why this fuss? It's only a game. If I keep thinking that I'll get hurt if I do this, or break my bones if I play that, I'll never have any fun. I could get hurt even without playing any games. Don't you think so? In my school, no one can swing as high as I can or jump from the swing like I do.'

'Enough, my child. I almost had a heart attack a while ago. Come home now. It's getting dark. Your mother will be angry if you don't do your homework. Where is your brother? Call him. Let's go home now.' Pankajakshi looked around for Sudhir.

'He went home long ago,' said Supriya, following her grandmother.

'Don't you ever repeat this feat again, Supriya,' warned Pankajakshi. 'You may break your hand or leg. Then there will be no point in wailing. By the way, when you play at school, don't any of your teachers supervise the games?'

'They are there Ammama. But I take care that no one sees me when I jump from the swing,' said Supriya, smiling at her grandmother's nervousness.

That night Pankajakshi lay awake thinking of her granddaughter and the swing.

She lived with her son in Madhya Pradesh. This was her

first visit to Delhi to her daughter's house. She had been born and brought up in a village. Her education was hardly worth a mention. As a child she had played only with dolls and dice and the toys that girls were meant to play with. But she had been especially fond of swinging. There was a tamarind tree in front of their house. Children from the neighbourhood had tied a rope to one of its lower branches, which functioned as a swing. Pankajakshi used to join them once in a while, but only when her father was not around. Her mother indulged the girl's fascination for the swing, but her father never allowed her to go anywhere near it. 'After all she is a girl. Suppose she breaks her limbs, how will she spend the rest of her life? Who will marry a lame girl?' was his argument. He had very strong ideas about how his daughter should behave: a girl should not be jumping and running around, she should be skillful at household work. 'If she is not disciplined as a child, how can she ever be disciplined as a woman?' he would query. 'A girl should walk so softly that even the sound of her footfall shouldn't be heard. She should be so humble as to fit into a ring without any disharmony.' Her father's word was law in that house. Nobody raised their voice, laughed loudly, sang songs or jumped on the terrace when he was at home. Everyone was serious and silent and went about their own work.

Pankajakshi followed all the rules. She had no problem in obeying them. She never questioned anybody about anything, nor did she feel it necessary to ask anyone why things were the way they were. But the swing was different. It always tempted her. She was too small to enjoy swinging when her brother was born, but by the time her sister arrived, the cradle in which the baby slept held a special attraction for her. The elders in the house used to chide her if they spotted her sitting in the huge wooden box-like cradle that hung from the ceiling, so she would often pretend she was swinging her sister and sit in the cradle

J. Bhagyalakshmi

herself. When no one was around, Pankajakshi used to sit on the edge of the cradle and swing. Sometimes, even without being aware of it, her hands would be on the rope even if she was not in the swing. When her sister grew up a little, however, the cradle vanished from the house.

Then her mother began objecting to her swinging on the rope on the tamarind tree as well. 'Do you think you are still a child to swing and be reckless? Look at Subhadramma's daughter. Look how good she is at household work! Her mother has all the time in the world to do whatever she likes. And just look at me. Such a grown-up girl at home, still I have no comfort. Sugunamma's daughter is very good at tailoring. She stitches clothes for everyone in her house. She also knows embroidery and knitting. Why don't you learn something from her? Tomorrow when you go to your in-laws' they will blame me for not teaching my daughter anything ...'

Pankajakshi got married when she was barely eighteen. The next year she had a baby boy. Two years later she had a baby girl and immersed herself totally in her home and children. The nature of her husband's job was such that the family had to live in cities and urban areas. Their life was thus limited to small dwellings. There were no large houses, or even the large compounds that Pankajakshi had been used to in the village. Her children did not have huge cradles hanging from ropes, both their cradles had stands.

But Pankajakshi's love for the swing remained intact. Perhaps it was not love, but a childhood longing that had frozen within her. Whenever she saw a swing, Pankajakshi's heart would be all a-flutter.

Once, she had attended a marriage at a relatives' house in a bigger town. The house was huge, with many rooms and all conceivable comforts. For Pankajakshi, the most fascinating thing there was a huge swing made out of a plank of wood hanging from the ceiling in the centre of the hall. She used to look at it longingly and dream of sitting on it at least for a few minutes. But the house was full of people and the swing was never free. Even during the nights someone or the other would be sleeping on it.

Then Pankajakshi decided that if they ever built a house for themselves, it would be big and airy, and would certainly have a swing in the middle of the hall. She would sit on the swing for as long as she pleased. After all, it would be her home and it would be under her management. Who would question her?

But Pankajakshi's dreams remained dreams, for building a house in the city was a most expensive affair. Even a medium-sized flat would cost a few lakhs. How could one have a large house, a big hall with a swing in it ... not in this birth at least. These things happened only in movies, not in real life. Pankajakshi soon realized this bitter truth and the swing remained a longing in her heart.

Whenever she took her children to the park, she used to put them on the swing and swing them slowly as though she were living her dream. Her children's shouts of 'Please Mummy, push harder, I want to swing faster' used to thrill her, but she would never sit on the swing herself. Would she not die of shame if someone asked, 'When there are so many children around, should you be swinging, Madam?'

Now she was in her daughter's house, and in the park right across the road were two swings, empty and inviting. Pankajakshi let out a sigh of helplessness. Her thoughts went back to Supriya. Today Supriya, a mere seven-year-old, her own granddaughter, had been swinging so freely and fearlessly, and she had jumped from such a great height. What pleasure did she get out of it, Pankajakshi wondered, admiring the girl's fearlessness and sense of adventure.

The little girl was to Pankajakshi a symbol of freedom, a reflection of hope, a flag of victory. Her own life had been like

J. Bhagyalakshmi

still water in a well whereas Supriya's was like a rushing brook. If she was like 'yesterday', Supriya was 'tomorrow'. The very thought gave a lot of satisfaction to Pankajakshi.

The whole night Pankajakshi lay awake, lost in her musings. She got up very early in the morning, washed her face and went to the park for a walk. There was no one around. She saw the swings moving in the cool breeze and beckoning her. Pankajakshi looked around to make sure no one was watching and suddenly sat down on a swing. Come what may, she thought. A shiver ran through her body. Laughter was bursting out of her. She closed her lips and tried to contain the laughter that bubbled within her stomach. At first she swung hesitantly, slowly. Then she increased her speed. She felt as if she were amidst the clouds, sailing on waves of bliss. What an experience! Her mind rushed back fifty years. She had become a child again. Her village ... the tamarind tree ... the swing ... she herself swinging happily ... Oh, what is happening, why is she going so high in spite of herself? Will she feel dizzy? Will she lose her grip? Will she fall? She closed her eyes tight.

Ripples of laughter, the touch of tender little hands and a voice, 'Ammama I will swing you very high. Don't be afraid. Just hold on tight. I'm here, just behind you. You are safe. Ready ... steady ... go'. Supriya started to push the swing gently as her grandmother threw her head back and laughed.

—*Translated from the Telugu by the author*

My Mother, Her Crime

Whenever I think of my mother, certain incidents flash through my mind and stab my heart.

My elder sister Kalyani has frequent fainting fits. I am not of an age to understand, being only four years old.

I open my eyes at dawn. Something sounds in my ears like the rhythmic striking of a drum. I go to the door to see. They have seated Kalyani on a wooden plank. Someone stands in front of her with a switch of leaves in his hand. My baby brother, whose gurgling laugh was to delight us for only four months, is in his cradle in my room.

'Nirajatchi, go and bring it now,' says someone.

I look at my mother.

I remember her dark blue sari. Her hair is gathered into a knot. Mother goes into the little room that is adjacent to mine. She removes the top part of her sari and collects breast milk into the little bowl that is in her hand. Tears spill from her eyes.

Every morning, while it is still dark, my mother lights the firewood under the big brass pot which is built into the bathroom, and heats the water.

I watch her one day. Her hair has come undone and hangs loose. She sits on her haunches, knees doubled. Her hair falls on her cheek and ears. As soon as the fire is alight, the red glow of the flames plays across my mother's lowered profile. That day she is wearing a red sari. Even as I am gazing at her, she quickly gets to her feet. Her hair falls down to her knees. Her sari has slipped and beneath her unhooked choli, I can see the green veins on her pale breasts. Suddenly she seems to me like the daughter of Agni who has come flying down from elsewhere. Could this be my mother? Really my mother?

Kali Kali Mahakali Bhadrakali
Namostute.

Why does the sloka come to mind all at once?

'Amma.'

My mother turns her head.

'What are you doing here, di?'

I cannot speak. My whole body is covered in sweat.

The sacred fire is lit in the house. Is it the redness of my mother's lips, or the sharp kumkumam mark on her forehead that makes her seem the very image of those blazing flames? With long drawn out 'Agniye Swaahaa,' they pour ghee on to the flames. And with each 'swaahaaa' my eyes dart from the fire to my mother.

My mother gives me an oil massage and bath. Her sari is lifted high and tucked up. I can see the smoothness of her light-skinned thighs. When she bends down and then stretches up, a green vein throbs there.

'Amma, how is it that you are so fair? How come I am dark?'

She laughs. 'Go on with you. Who can be as beautiful as you are?'

There is no connection between these incidents, except that my mother is queen in all of them. She was the purifying fire that burnt away all impurities. With a single smile, she created a million beauties that seemed to hang like pennants in my mind. When I lay with my head on her lap, she would stroke me with her long, cool fingers and say quite ordinary things like, 'I am going to send you to dance classes. You have a fine body.' Or she would say, 'Such lovely hair, di.' Trivial things. But immediately something would flower in my heart.

Now I am not sure whether these feelings were of her instigation, or because of some quite independent imagination of my own. And I don't know what she intended to create for herself when she sowed these seeds in me.

I am thirteen. My paavaadais are all getting too short for me. My mother has to lengthen each one of them.

One evening, as I lie with my head on my mother's lap, some words I had read earlier, come to mind.

'Amma, what does "puberty" mean?'

Silence.

A long silence.

Suddenly she says, 'Always be as you are now, running about and playing, twirling your skirt ...'

Some people are to visit my aunt's house, to 'see' her daughter, Radhu, for a possible marriage. My mother too goes away there. So on this eventful day she is not at home: it is my sister who rubs me with oil and washes my hair. Through the bathroom window I can see the still dark sky.

'Kalloos, you've woken me up far too early. I can't even hear the sound of fireworks.'

'After your oil massage and bath, I've got to do mine, haven't I? You are thirteen years old now. Can't even do your own hair. Lower your head, stupid.'

Kalyani has no patience.

She rubs my head until it hurts, as if she is pulling away the

Ambai

fibres from a coconut shell.

For that particular Dipavali, my mother has made me a paavaadai of purple satin. How I had yearned for it as it slithered smoothly under the sewing machine! This time she had measured me carefully before she began.

'Come here child, I have to measure you. You've definitely grown taller.' She measures me and then looks up. 'This girl has grown taller by two inches.'

This purple satin paavaadai was not going to be too short. It was sure to glide right down to reach the floor.

Abruptly Kalyani pulls me to my feet and rubs my hair dry. I pull on my chemise and run to the puja room. My father hands me my set of new clothes from the ones stacked on the plank.

'Here you are, dark girl.' He always called me that.

I go back inside, calling out to my sister, 'Kalloos ...' Basket in hand I stand in front of her saying, 'I've gone and stained my new skirt all over. Will Amma scold me?'

Kalyani gives me a horrified stare for a full minute and then goes off screaming, 'Appa!'

That look, and the way she runs off, without so much as taking the basket from me send centipedes crawling in my mind. I glance at the satin skirt. I run my hand over the velvet jacket.

Nothing has happened, has it?

Good God, nothing has happened to me, has it? But even as I ask myself this, I realize that something has indeed happened. Everywhere about me there is the thunderous noise of exploding fireworks. I stand there, clutching the flower basket, my breath coming in gasps, lips trembling, shaking all over.

With a great sob the tears come.

I want my mother. I want to bury my head deep into the Chinnalampatti silk of her shoulder. I want, unashamed, to tell her, 'I am frightened.' I want her to comfort me and stroke my head. Because, surely, something very terrible has happened.

Kalyani brings along the shaven-headed old widow from next door who helps with jobs like making murukku. This old woman comes up to me.

'What are you crying about, you silly girl? What has happened after all? Nothing the whole world doesn't know about.'

I cannot follow a word of what she is saying. Nothing seems to reach my understanding, although my instinct, half grasping something, freezes in fear. I feel a single desperate need from the depth of my being, like an unquenchable thirst. Amma ...

I remember the time I was lost, when I was five years old. I am walking along a huge park, oblivious of the gathering darkness. Then all of a sudden, the darkening trees loom; the noises and the silences begin to frighten me. My father finds me, but it is not until I see my mother that the tears come bursting out.

My mother takes me to her side. She strokes me and says softly, 'There! Nothing whatever has happened to you. Everything is all right now.' Her lips are like blades of flame when she puts her face against mine.

Now too I am struck with that same fear, as if I am lost.

I sink down, bury my head against my knees and weep. I feel as if something has ended for ever. As if I have left something behind, in the way one leaves the cinema after they show 'The End' on the screen. It seems to me that in all human history I am alone in my sadness. I weep as if I carry all the world's sorrows on my own narrow velvet-clad shoulders.

I wonder why my mother never spoke to me of these things when we were together in the evenings.

My mind is pervaded with fear. It isn't even the kind of fright that grips one because of alien surroundings or unknown people. No, this is like the absolute terror and confusion that assaults one at mid-scream, seconds after seeing a snake. Such terror hangs, like spiders' webs, from all corners of my mind.

I remember seeing a corpse with pale lips split apart. The head had smashed against a stone. A moment before, a bald pink head had been in front of me. Now it was split open like the mouth of a cave, and gushing dark red blood. Within minutes, the blood dripped to the ground. I started at it. The redness spread everywhere and seemed to leap into my eyes. Now these repelling images return. So much blood. So much blood—but no sound comes from my mouth. A bed of blood. The old man opens his mouth. The eyes stare open. They bore into my heart. Blood is so frightful … enough to make lips pale and limbs freeze.

I need my mother. My heart yearns for her to free me from this fear and ugliness.

'Please, why don't you get up. How much longer will you keep crying?' Kalyani begs. She is sitting next to me and has been crying too.

'Amma …'

'But you know she's coming back next week. I've just written to her about all this. She'll come as soon as Radhu's "viewing" is over. Get up now. This is becoming a real headache.' Kalyani is getting angry.

'What has happened to me?'

'Nothing. Your skull. How many times do I have to tell you?'

'Am I not allowed to climb trees after this?'

She gives me a swift blow on the head.

'Fathead! Here I've been begging you for the last half hour to come and change your clothes, and you've got to be asking all these questions. Appa!' She calls out to my father, 'She's being a terrible nuisance.'

My father comes and says, 'You mustn't be difficult now. You must do as Kalyani says.'

And after he goes away, the old widow adds, 'Why does she have to be so stubborn? This is every woman's destiny, after all.'

Seven days. Seven days for Mother to come home after they have 'seen' Radhu. Seven days of stumbling in the dark.

One day the women from the neighbouring houses come to visit.

'Shouldn't she be wearing a davani now, Kalyani?'

'Only after my mother returns, maami. She's terribly wilful. She only listens to Amma.'

'O, she'll be all right hereafter. Hereafter she'll be modest, She'll know what is proper.'

Why?

What is going to happen hereafter?

Why should I wear a davani? Didn't Amma say, 'Always be the same as you are now, twirling your skirt ...' Why should I change?

Nobody explains. They make me sit here like a doll and gossip among themselves. When my father comes in, they draw their saris tightly about themselves and lower their voices.

On the fifth day, Kalyani gives me warmed oil in a bowl. 'From now on, you had better do your own oil massage,' she says.

Weeping, I battle with my waist-length hair, and then stand in front of the hall mirror in my chemise.

'Finish dressing in the bathroom hereafter. Understand?' says my father.

I close the door after him and remove my chemise. The mirror reflects to me my own dark body. My hands run by turns over my shoulders, arms, my chest, my waist and my soft thighs, all of them very slightly paler than my face. Then am I not the same girl as I was? What is my mother going to say? I put on my school uniform.

As soon as I open the door, Kalyani comes in. 'What are you going to tell them at school when they ask you why you've been absent?'

I stare at her. I had been about to set off for school with the exultation of a bird that has just been released from its cage, but now my spirit is dashed.

'You don't have to say anything. Just keep quiet.'

I don't join in during the games lesson. I hide behind a large tree. Once before I had done this and Miss Leela Menon asked us in class the next day, 'Who are the fools who didn't play yesterday?'

I didn't stand up.

'And you? Why aren't you on your feet?' she asked.

'I am not a fool, Miss,' I replied. She wrote in my progress report that I am impertinent.

But today I don't even fear Miss Leela Menon's scolding—it strikes me that nothing will ever be more important to me than this one thing that has happened to me now. I don't want to sit under the tree and read Enid Blyton as I usually do. I ask the dry leaves that have fallen into a hole by the tree, 'What on earth has happened to me?'

I look forward to my mother's answer with the anxiety of an accused who waits upon the pronouncement of a judge.

Will Amma say, lowering her eyes and looking at me, 'This thing that has happened to you is beautiful too'? I know that by the fiery spark of her smile she will get rid of all of them: the old woman who frightened me, Kalyani, all. My mother is different from all of them. Where she stands there is no place for unnecessary things. Everything is essentially beautiful to her.

I need her desperately. There is something yet to be explained. Someone has to explain to me gently why my whole body sweats and trembles at the mere thought of the purple satin skirt; why all of a sudden my tongue goes as dead as a piece of wood; why the world seems to darken and before I can turn to look I hear that terrible exploding noise and see streaming blood and a long corpse.

I sense that everyone has gone and I am alone. The gardener wakes me up. Slowly I go home.

'Why are you so late, girl? Where did you go?'

'Nowhere. I was sitting under the tree.'

'Alone?'

'Mmm.'

'What is the matter with you? Do you imagine you are still a little girl? Supposing something were to happen ...'

I throw down my satchel. My face feels very hot. Putting my hands over my ears, I shriek, 'Yes, I will sit there like that. Nothing is wrong with me.'

It's a crazy shriek, each word drawn out into a scream. My father and Kalyani stand there, stunned.

In a great fury, I rush past them upstairs, and sit on the open terrace. I want to stay alone in the scent of the champakam. Neither Kalyani nor my father should ever come up here. This scent which is without words or touch is more comforting to me than the people of this house. How pleasant it would be if they never, never spoke. Why can't they just smile with that widening of the eyes, like my mother? When she smiles like that, something happens inside me. I want to break out into laughter. I want to sing. She is an artist, a creator. With a turn of the head and a smile she can summon joy, enthusiasm, beauty. Like magic.

Kalyani comes upstairs.

'Come and eat, your highness. Amma has spoilt you rotten and no mistake.'

I stand up nonchalantly and look at her in scorn.

My mother comes home the next day. She opens the taxi door and walks into the house, her sari of dark green silk creased from the journey.

'What happened?' asks my father.

'He's refused, the rascal. Apparently the girl is too dark-skinned.'

'What does your sister say?'

'She grieves, naturally. Poor thing.'

'We too have a dark girl.'

I dash down to stand in front of her. I want to explain everything to her myself, much better than Kalyani did in her letter. I want to tell her about all the creeping horrors. I want to pour it all out into the crook of her neck, quietly, with trembling mouth.

I look deeply into her eyes, sure that now, at last, she is going to explain the mystery; the feelings that choke my throat at night, my distress at the changes in my own body. She is just about to take me into the circle of her arms. I know I shall weep out aloud. I shall twist my fingers into her hair and let the loud sobs come bursting out.

She looks at me.

I don't know whether in that instant I am changed into another Radhu.

Her words are like a sting. 'And what a time for this wretched business of yours! It's just one more burden for us now.'

Whom is she accusing?

Noiseless sobs knock at my chest.

A blood-red glow spits out from my mother's lips and her nostrils and her kumkumam mark and her nose-drop and her eyes. In that fiery instant the divine image that covered her falls away to reveal the mere, the human mother. Her cold unfeeling words rise like swords blindly butchering all the beauties that she had hitherto tended. Endless fears will stay forever in my mind from now on; dark pictures.

My Mother, Her Crime   91

Agniye swaahaa. Not impurities alone are burnt in the fire.
Buds and blossoms too are blackened.

—*Translated from the Tamil by Lakshmi Holmström*

Ambai

Pratibha Ray

Mushi

Even today, when the season for blue water-lilies arrives, I see Mushi's dark face mirrored in the shallow rippling water. What connection could there be between Mushi and blue water-lilies, anyone listening to her story might ask mockingly.

Ages have slipped by since Mushi's passing. Even so, to me it is like yesterday, because her face, dark as the seeds of a gourd, is bright in my memory in this season, when even a palmful of water, dripping into a hollow, will make blue water-lilies sprout in an instant.

There never was an occasion for anyone to photograph Mushi. So it will be necessary to sketch her out for you before I begin my tale.

'The colour of the seeds of a gourd,' one says when describing someone. Only in Mushi's case, it was no figure of speech. If you were to stand behind her and scatter a handful of those seeds over her bare back, it would be difficult, even in broad daylight, to gather them in again. You couldn't distinguish eyes, nose, lips from forehead in that jetblack face. Which is a blessing, for if you could, would you even look at her?

Since her hair was a few shades lighter than her forehead, it was possible to make out, although with difficulty, the straggling strands which hung below her neck in wispy mouse-tails, a cubit and half in length, sometimes in braids as thick as the fruits of the drumstick tree, or else twisted into a swaying knot. Her eyelashes and eyebrows were hairless. Could you have spotted them if they had been thicker or if she had darkened them with lamp-black? The limbs could have been polished granite if only Mushi had been more sleek or if oil and turmeric had touched her skin. But her body, smeared with mud, dust and cowdung from her unending labours, was bleached ash-gray, like the fabric of an umbrella left out in the sun. Only her glistening teeth stood out, so bright that they looked out of place. When she smiled you saw not just the rows of dazzling teeth but the gums as well, the colour of half-roasted brinjals. Which was why her smile looked so grotesque despite those pearl-like teeth. For jewellery she wore a tiny neem twig in her nose and a black thread round her neck. You could make out the twig of neem, which stood out like a pole, but not the thread. It was as if it wasn't there.

What did Mushi wear? She was wrapped in a length of filthy coarse homespun, and was bare from the knees down. Bare above the waist too—but which girl of Mushi's age and status wore a blouse in those days? I can't remember Mushi ever using turmeric, oil, lamp-black or sindoor. All I remember is her filth-stained hands patting cowdung into cakes. Hands that oozed mud and cowdung as she plastered the courtyard of her hut. Unwashed she was from the day she was born. Each time I saw Mushi she was busy chopping, grinding, scrubbing. In those days I was never troubled by the thought that Mushi had to work so hard. Because just as I spent my time going to school, returning, visiting neighbours' homes, playing, creating mischief, so too did Mushi keep herself busy gathering cowdung, leaves, firewood, getting scolded and beaten. My life was natural to me and Mushi's to her.

How shall I describe my relationship with Mushi? Friend,

classmate, peer—her equal in age and status? No, none of these. 'No one' can be a relationship too, the deepest and most intimate of relationships, which one cannot understand at the time but only later, when the experience has sunk into you, when you grope for a hand but cannot find it.

Keli Gouduni delivered milk at our door early each morning. When one got up bleary-eyed with sleep, there was the pot of foaming milk and the toothy grin on Keli Gouduni's dark face. Her affection was as wholesome as the milk.

When she saw me with my face unwashed she would widen her toothy smile and say: 'Chhi, Dei how lazy you are! Look how high the sun is, and you are getting up now? Our Mushi got up when it was still dark and has already swept and washed the yard with cowdung water, gathered two armfuls of dew-soaked bamboo leaves for the fire and parboiled a pot of paddy, cleaned out the cowshed, mashed yams and tubers into a chutney for her father's morning meal, while I delivered milk to customers. Hurry up, brush your teeth and drink up the milk! Do school-children sleep so late?'

Had Mushi really finished so many chores so early in the morning? How old was she after all? If she was three years older than me, she would be thirteen at best.

Who could have said she was a child of twelve or thirteen? She was a woman from the day she was born. If you are a girl child in a poor household you have had it! You will never have childhood, adolescence, or youth. You'll transform straight from a child into a woman!

Mushi was spending her childhood as a woman while I, only a child, savoured her womanhood. At that age one loves to play in the mud, to roam about unwashed in dirty clothes, hair loose and streaming with lice. In the scorching afternoons I pretended to be asleep behind closed doors, though sleep never came, for fear of Mother's scolding. Thus was my childhood restrained. I yearned to wander away in the hot sun, hands filthy with cowdung like Mushi's. How happy she was, my child's mind said. While for me it was: up early and off too school! Bathe at the right time; comb your hair; put on clean clothes; drink up your milk. Lessons to be completed in the evenings while heads nodded drowsily. And again, don't go out in the sun, don't get wet. 'No, no, no' to everything that you could have enjoyed. In those days, who knows why, I felt a craving to do everything that was forbidden by my parents or Nata Master, our schoolteacher. Being routine-bound from morning to evening, I was fascinated by things that lay beyond those routines. Mushi has no routines, I thought: there is nothing she must do at the right time. True, she has to get up at some unearthly hour, but she brushes her teeth at the wrong time, bathes, eats, sleeps at wrong times. What fun she has! How could the child's mind understand that everything Mushi did followed a routine too? Not a routine of her own making. She was driven by the routine of poverty that made up her parents' lives.

Though Mushi was older I called her by name and though I was younger she addressed me as 'Dei' (elder sister). When I had to describe her to my schoolmates I said, 'Mushi, you know, Keli Gouduni's daughter! That black girl with lice in her hair. Now do you know who I mean?' And when Mushi spoke of me to *her* friends she said, 'That's our Dei, our babu's daughter. She goes to school, sings beautifully. Slim as a doll.' Her words never made me puff up with pride. Utterly natural, those words that each one used to introduce a trusted friend. There was no disdain in my words, nor any hint of defence in hers. She knew how close I was to her and I was confident of her intimacy.

Next to our school compound was the mud hut in which Ghana Gouda, the milkman, lived. The two outer rooms of the hut comprised the cowshed, through which one reached the courtyard facing which were the rooms of Ghana Gouda, his wife Keli Gouduni, their daughter Mushi and son Tinka. At one end of the courtyard was the dhenki used to husk paddy. The kitchen lay at the other end. Since my father was the Headmaster, we occupied quarters inside the school compound. Our house, therefore, was at one end of the compound and Mushi's at the other. Along the edges of the school compound were the bastis of the Muslims, the chamars, the washermen and the other castes. These were our neighbours and friends. The Brahmins, Karnas and other high-caste people lived some three or four kilometres away. That was the village proper. Which was why my closest and dearest friend was Mushi.

As soon as I came from school I would shove a few morsels of food down my throat and hop away like a bird to Mushi's home. She would be busy with her chores, and I followed her around and watched. At that age one's hands and feet are constantly itching for action. Mushi would gather varieties of saag from the fields and the embankments lining the ponds and tuck them away in the folds of her sari around the waist. I walked behind her, stopping, clumsily plucking all kinds of wild grass and leaves, which I thrust into her waist-cloth. Sometimes, when I saw a worm or caterpillar, I would scream in horror and hold on to Mushi. Occasionally, when my hands became muddy, I would wipe them on her bare back. Mushi remained unperturbed, as if it was a wall, not her back. That was my game!

Mushi would interrupt her harvesting and carefully separate the rubbish I had picked from the saag. With a sweet smile she would say, 'Dei, you will never learn! Can't you recognize what is edible and what isn't, even though you have been coming to the fields with me everyday? All you do is to add to my work. Ba will be coming home from the ploughing any time now. How will he eat his meal unless I fry some of this saag for him?'

Hurriedly, she would clean and wash the saag, light a twig fire and set the clay pot over it. When it was hot enough, she would pour into it a few drops of grimy-looking mustard oil out of the narrow-mouthed bottle which hung from a nail on the wall by a strand of thread. She added a bit of chilli and a few mustard seeds for taste and upturned the washed saag leaves into the pot. And instantly, the surroundings grew fragrant with the smell! None of the food at home ever smelt like that. I would sniff up that fragrance so powerfully that my nostrils collapsed like a balloon from which the air had escaped. That smell went straight into my entrails. I wondered how Mushi had become such a good cook at that tender age. Anything that she dumped into her cooking pot smelled divine! On some days she would smile and say, 'Dei, would you like to taste a bit of our saag? You won't lose your caste if you eat our food. We are cowherds. Krishna was of our caste, you know. The only difference is that we are poor …'

When she said this Mushi's dark, expressionless face turned a little pale. Attaching no importance to all this, I would scoop a little saag out of her bowl, eat it, and then wipe my hands on my frock. Mushi would say 'Dei, why are you always in such a hurry? Did you have to eat from my bowl? I could have got a fresh bowl for you! My mother will be angry if she finds out.' My classmates were girls from different castes. We would each bring different kinds of condiments from home—mashed tamarind, sour mango kernels and what not— and during playtime we would pool everything together into a stone bowl I fetched from home and snatch the delicacies from each other's fingers. Some girl would snatch away a mango kernel that another girl had been sucking and lick it, making appreciative noises. We had no fear of defilement then. Why would I hesitate to share Mushi's food now? The dunce! Didn't she know that you couldn't lose caste by eating with a friend?

Mushi would take a rag, dripping with mud and moist cowdung, and plaster the large courtyard of their home with infinite care. She would squat, reaching out as far as she could, stretch her arm, raise herself on her toes and swivel around in a circle, making cloud patterns on the wet mud. She slid backwards along the courtyard as she worked, while I walked barefoot across the floor, leaving a trail of footprints. She would laugh and say, 'Dei, you are ruining everything!' But she made no attempt to wipe my footprints away; instead, she would loosen the end of her sari, which she had tucked in at her waist, and wipe the mud and cowdung off my feet. I would immediately get them muddy again. This was my favourite game. During the long school vacation, most of my time was spent with Mushi. When it was time to bathe or eat, someone would come and drag me home, against my will. Best of all was the season when the millets ripened for harvest. Straw were piled outside the house for the cows to eat and ears of ripe grain lay in another pile. Mushi's house, and even her filthy clothes and her untidy hair, would be suffused with the slightly sweet smell of ripe millets. Mushi would break the stems into finger-lengths which she chewed and gave me to chew. How sweet they were— younger brothers to sugar cane! But I preferred to inhale the scent of ripe millets. I also loved the smell of the leaves of turmeric plants which were cut from the plants and piled outside Mushi's door. The smells in Mushi's house changed with the seasons. Sometimes it was the steamy scent of parboiled rice, sometimes the odour of burnt molasses; at other times the smell of smoke from cowdung fires or the smell of boiling milk or yoghurt or cream. Our house had no such smells.

Another reason for my intimacy with Mushi was her willingness to stand by me in all my indiscretions and misadventures. In the settlement of the low-caste bauris, someone was being tormented by a female spirit just when

Kuntala, the washerman's wife, was heard making strange roaring sounds behind closed doors, thus confirming the widely-held suspicion that she was a live witch.

These places were prohibited to me, but I could tell Mother that I was going to Mushi's house and slip away. However, I was too timid to go alone. Mushi had to drop all her work and accompany me to the bauri settlement and then to the washermen's basti. When she returned home she was taken to task for neglecting her chores, all because of me. But neither of us cared. A wedding in the Muslim basti; a violent quarrel in the chamar settlement; a death in a Muslim household where everyone was worried about how the corpse could fit into the white bag-like shroud whose mouth had to be sewn up and how it was to be buried—I was eager to see all these sights, forbidden to someone of my age. But what fear did I have when Mushi was around? She would come quietly and give me the information. Then the two warriors would sally forth. But that night neither of us could sleep a wink. I would cling to Mother all night and try to pass on to her, through contact, more than half of my own fear. When she snored, I would shake her awake and ask, 'Mother, where does one go after death? Is one born again from the same mother's womb? And if one is born elsewhere, does one still remember one's mother and father? I shall be your daughter again if I die, shan't I? Mother, mother, why don't you say yes? I feel so frightened when you fall asleep.' I would give her another shake. She would ask in a drowsy voice 'What are you afraid of?' 'I went with Mushi to the Muslim house to see the corpse.' And again I would grab her tightly.

When Keli came the next morning with the milk, Mother would complain at once, 'Does Mushi have no sense at all? Taking the child to a place like that! She is prone to all kinds of fears, you know; she had lost an elder as well as a younger sister. What if something had happened? Tell Mushi, such a thing should not be repeated.'

Mushi was severely punished on my account. 'Look, Yama (the god of Death) may have no desire to carry off such a worthless creature as you, but our Dei is a delicate child, easily scared. What if she had got frightened? Would you have managed her?' But Mushi was used to all this. Beatings and scoldings slid off her back like floating clouds. The moment she heard of another exciting event she would find a way for both of us to be there.

But it was the blue water-lilies that brought us closest. When the rains came the flowers beckoned from hollows and puddles, nodding to me, winking, tickling. On a Saturday or Sunday Mushi and I would venture forth on our quest. Water-lilies do not grow in all places; they choose spots which are hard to find. But each day Mushi would bring news of new places where water-lilies were blooming. To me, that was the greatest thrill of all. If on some days I wasn't able to go out Mushi would somehow bring me a bunch of the flowers with their long stems intact. I would float the flowers in a bucket of water and sit watching them. Studies would be forgotten. If Mother asked me for a flower for her puja I would refuse to part with even one of them. Didn't she know they would wilt if they were taken out of the water?

I had an excuse handy too. 'How can you offer these flowers to your gods?' I would say. 'When Mushi plucked them, she hadn't bathed. They are unclean!'

'That doesn't matter when the flowers are for the gods.' Mother would reply. 'Don't girls go out early in the morning to gather flowers for the Khudurkuni festival? They haven't even brushed their teeth then!'

'Yes, but do you know where these flowers were growing? In the little pond by the meadow where people go to ease themselves. That's where the Muslims wash their bottoms!'

'So what? Neither the pond nor the caste can defile a flower. Don't you know that the lotus grows out of mud?'

Finally, helpless, I had to seek refuge in Mushi. 'Mother, Mushi made me swear on my books that I would only play with these flowers, not use them for puja or give them to you. If I break my vow I shall never do well in my studies.'

Somehow, the flowers never reached Mother's hands. But it was Mushi who had to face the consequences.

'Who asked Mushi to bring flowers? What right does she have to impose such a vow on the child over such a small thing? Does that stupid girl know how difficult it is to get knowledge from books? All right, let her come today ...'

Such quarrels involving Mushi and me were common. Sometimes Keli would come with an accusation: 'Ma, I know you will say I am carrying tales against the child. After all, if Dei eats a couple of guavas from our tree, it won't run out of fruit. Why, bats are eating away heaps of our guavas everyday! But Dei has not only been climbing the tree and plucking the fruits, she has been shaking the tender blossoms off the branches! We are poor folk. If we could sell the guavas in the haat that would pay for the vegetables we buy.' Before Mother could say a word I would jump in with my defence: 'I asked Mushi if I could climb the tree. I never go even to the foot of that tree for fear of hairy caterpillars, but Mushi told me there are no caterpillars this time. "Why don't you climb up?" Mushi told me, "Nothing will happen." It was Mushi who showed me the ripe guavas. I could not climb up to the higher branches. Mushi said if I shook the branches the guavas would drop off. So that's what I did. Is it my fault if the blossoms dropped off along with the fruit?' Mother would pay Keli some money to compensate her for the loss, and hand out a reprimand to Mushi along with a scolding to me. 'She's just a child, how could Mushi advise her to climb trees? What if she had fallen and broken a limb? Girls have to be careful!'

Another drubbing for Mushi.

Mushi had no friends at all. Boys wouldn't look at her and even girls kept away, refusing to touch her on the shoulder for the games that girls play during the Kuanr Punei festival, as though her dark colour would rub off on them or the smell of cowdung be transferred to their bodies.

Did Mushi have time for friends? She even had to pay for the little time she spent with me because her mother said she was neglecting her duties. But she never left me and I never left her.

Then one day I heard Mushi's marriage had been fixed. The groom worked in Kolkata and earned a handsome salary. He looked like a prince, everyone said. Fair-skinned, with dagger-sharp features, tall and slim. However did he agree to marry Mushi?

The boy had never set eyes on Mushi. Neither had his parents. They had been attracted by Mushi's reputation of being hardworking. They needed someone to take care of the house. What were good looks worth anyway; could you grind them into a powder and drink them up? That was what the matchmaker explained.

Keli Gouduni's feet hardly touched the earth now. She had always thought her Mushi would remain unmarried—a burden, hanging from her parents' necks. Tinka was their only son, five years younger than Mushi. Mushi had brought him up like a son, denying herself food so that he could eat, pandering to all his whims. Now he was inconsolable because his 'nani' (sister) was leaving. Would the ties remain just as firm when he found a wife? Anyway, they would be relieved of her soon.

When I heard about Mushi's bridegroom I was more excited than she. I abandoned my studies. I was constantly at Mushi's side, singing her bridegroom's praises to her. All that Keli said to my mother in his praise was repeated to her, with many additions. My goal: to see the moon rise in Mushi's face. But hers was the face of dark night. Let alone the moon, not even a star appeared in that sky. Was she wood or stone? Which girl wouldn't be thrilled when she heard her bridegroom's praises— particularly when he was a wage-earner from Kolkata?

I had planned to enjoy Mushi's wedding to the fullest, but when I woke up one morning there was Keli with the pot of milk, wiping her eyes. Mushi had left for her in-laws' home the night before. How could that be? There were no fireworks, no music—when did the bridegroom arrive, when was the wedding performed? I jumped out of bed and cross-examined her.

Wiping her eyes Keli said, 'No, Dei, those things are not for us. Can we dream of a wedding where the bride leaves in a palanquin? Ours was a tola-kania wedding; Mushi left last night with her father and brother for her in-laws' home. It's a long journey on foot, so night was the best time to go.'

All my hopes were drowned. Chii, do you call that a wedding? When the bride has to walk to the bridegroom's home but the bridegroom can't come to hers?

Keli said, 'He'll come, Dei, he'll come. All sons-in-law come to their in-laws' homes for the Gamha Punei festival. That's when all of us can see him. I just can't believe that my Mushi was fated to get a husband like a prince. But when her father and brother return we'll know what's true and what's not. Do you think I trust the matchmaker's words so far?'

Ghana and Tinka returned. That matchmaker doesn't know his job, they said. Why, the bridegroom is ten times more handsome than the matchmaker claimed he was! Who could describe his looks adequately?

Ghana was sorry that this princely son-in-law of his had to be married to an ugly, dark-skinned girl like Mushi. So what if she was his own daughter? Hadn't God given him eyes to see? In Ghana's opinion, Mushi was not worthy even to be her husband's handmaiden.

Mother asked, with some hesitation, 'Your son-in-law is loving to her, isn't he?'

Keli's toothy laugh could have pierced the onlooker like a needle. 'Just look at *my* face, Ma. Well, I set up a home and had children, didn't I? Where is the time for love in a house of sorrow? If you can find a handful to eat, something to wear, become the mother of sons and daughters, that's enough ...'

But for some reason Mother let out a long sigh. I was unable to think deeply then. All I could think of was how Mushi looked in her wedding ornaments, feeling cheated because I hadn't been able to see her.

My schooldays were about to end. Mushi had been away for six months now. I had no time to think of her because of the pressure of studies. One day I heard she was back in her father's home. She would be sent back later to her in-laws with due ceremony.

As soon as school was over I rushed to Mushi.

Had she really been married?

There were no ornaments on her body. The same neem twig was on her nose and the same black thread round her neck. There were two bunches of cheap glass bangles round her wrists, she was wearing the same filthy piece of coarse homespun, a round spot of sindoor on her forehead—that was all the evidence of marriage. Mushi was back at all her old chores, but she looked a little thicker round the waist. Her in-laws must have fed her well—poor thing!

Keli had a good laugh over this. 'Really, Ma, our Dei will never grow up,' she said. 'If she had been of our caste she would have been married by now. Mushi's marriage was delayed only because of her looks. And Dei asked her "Why have you become so fat in the stomach, Mushi? Your husband must have been feeding you well. Rasagollas from Kolkata?" '

'How many months?' Mother asked.

'Six months since she was married and she is five months gone. How long was our son-in-law at home anyway? Just the one month of leave that he had for the wedding. He hasn't returned since he left. And now we are told he can't come for Gamha Punei either. What can one do? One must think of one's job first. Is Kolkata so near that one can come whenever one likes? It's so far that even a bus can't go there, let alone a bullock cart. You have to go by train!' Keli's small eyeballs bulged so much that I was frightened. They seemed about to drop out! Keli had never seen a train but she had heard of them. For her, that was the conveyance of 'sahibs'! Her son-in-law travelled by train and that, to her, was the supreme glory.

Now Mushi no longer called me when someone died in the Muslim basti, nor did she go there herself. If there was a commotion in someone's house, Mushi heard nothing.

She never stepped into a pond or puddle to pluck water-lilies anymore. I felt her heart had turned more wooden than before. Her husband never came. She grew thicker with each passing day. Now she was unable to do any work.

Then Mushi gave birth to a son. She had a painful time of it. There was no blood in her; she nearly died. She smiled when she saw her son. They said this was the first time she had smiled since she had been married. All right, so she had given birth to a son! But don't so many others do it? What was there to smile about? How shameless of her! The women who had come to see the baby turned their faces away. True, it had a milk-white complexion, like a new-born calf. But wasn't she dark herself? That was why she was showing off!

The matriculation examination hovered overhead, but still I rushed to see Mushi's son. And true enough, I found it hard to believe that such a child had come out of her belly. Like a tender palmyra shoot growing out of an old, wrinkled kernel.

When I praised the boy Mushi said, 'He's a cheat, just like his father! He almost ripped me when he was born, but does he have even a trace of me?'

This was her glory, not an accusation. Her dark face lit up with the sheer pride of motherhood. I was happy too—not on account of the child, but because Mushi was happy. I had never seen such fulfilling joy in her before.

Mushi's husband came down from Kolkata when he got the news. I couldn't help feeling sad when I saw him. What a match for so handsome a boy! Who could say he was born in a cowherd family? His dress and speech matched his looks. If one didn't know he was a worker in a jute mill, one could have mistaken him for a gentleman. He saw the child and left some money for it. Making sure that Mushi could hear, he told his mother-in-law, 'I shall send money each month. Take good care of the child. I am the only son of my parents; this child will continue our line. We have no doctor in our village. There will be no one to look after them in Kolkata, when I go out to work. So they will have to be here for some time.'

Mushi sat holding the baby in her lap, eyes downcast, her tousled hair giving her the appearance of a ghostess. She hadn't seen her husband's face and he hadn't looked at her face when he talked. The son-in-law left without even having warmed a chair! Mushi and her son would remain in her father's home for an indefinite period. Just those few days she had spent with her husband—that was all she knew of marriage. Thereafter, she was passing her days proudly as a mother. No one saw her pining for her god-like husband. She worked as busily as a tumbler-pigeon, giving her son all the love in the world.

Every two or three months, there was a money order from Kolkata for the boy. Mushi merely put her thumbprint on the receipt. It was Tinka who received the money. For he was now master of the house. Ghana had grown old. Tinka was married. Mushi knew that her son was getting exactly the same food after the money had come as he would have got otherwise. Keli and Ghana were bald tree-trunks now, without branch or leaf; even if the winds blew, they could not stir.

Sabi, Tinka's wife, was forever nagging Mushi. Mushi wasn't doing her share of the work—her poor husband had to plough, weed, harvest, everything. The old man and his wife did go out to the fields, but there was little they could do.

Now Mushi started going to the fields too. She went out in the morning and returned in the evening. Her son, Udiya, was getting neglected, but Mushi never opened her mouth. Once he started going to school her sorrows would end.

Tinka said not a word to his sister or his wife. Sometimes he would buy sweets or snacks for Udiya and, occasionally, even clothes. Mushi ignored Sabi's taunts, since her brother gave so much affection to the child.

But Sabi continued to nag and grumble. Why was Tinka carrying the burden of someone else's wife and son? Would this never end? Would the son-in-law in Kolkata really come back for this ugly hag? Sometimes she nagged so much that Tinka had to raise a fist. That was Mushi's whole strength. Tinka was protecting her son and her.

But when Tinka shoved his wife violently into the house one day, Mushi could not bear it. It wasn't right to beat up a wife for the sake of a sister! Mushi was about to follow them into the house to intervene on her sister-in-law's behalf when her feet went numb. She was unable to move. Was Tinka saying such things to calm his wife? If that was the case, Mushi was safe. He was whispering to her, 'How stupid you are! Do you think Nani doesn't work for her food? She does the work of three men in the fields! It's more than enough to pay for her food as well as that of the child. Besides, it's because they are here that we are getting all that cash! I am depositing the money which that whoremonger sends from Kolkata in my account in the post office. When we have a son we'll need money for his education. If she decides to send the boy away because of your nagging, you'll be clashing your empty bowls together!'

Mushi's eyes filled up. They didn't overflow easily; she was used to sorrow. But these few words from Tinka left her shattered.

She wasn't hurt because Tinka had referred to her husband as a patron of prostitutes. What had hurt her was that the lid had come off his hollow brotherly love. What treachery lay hidden behind that lid! The day those money orders from Kolkata stopped, she would be a stranger in her own father's house.

Mushi stayed on, never saying a word. She was working harder than ever before on her brother's fields so that he would take pity on her.

I had, by now, completed school and was a boarder in a college hostel. Whenever I came home I would meet Mushi. Her son was the great attraction. She said very little. I felt she had allowed herself to age in these few years for no reason at all. Her husband came once a year. He brought clothes, toys and food for the child. He would stay a few hours and go back. Tinka never asked him to stay on; as for Ghana, he was as good as crippled. No one was keen to keep him: there would be all kinds of formalities and expenses. Mushi couldn't ask him to stay for a day or two. She herself was a burden on her brother. Her husband had no interest in staying either. Although they had hardly spoken to each other, in those fifteen days they spent together she had read his mind. A woman might know little of the world outside, but the mere look on a man's face will tell her how much value she has for him. What claim did she have to ask him to stay the night? Looks she might lack, but not a woman's instinct.

Udiya had not grown used to his father and did not go to him when he was called. His father's visits made no difference to the child. He clung to Mushi like a leech. Mushi lived for Udiya and Udiya for Mushi; their entire world was made up of each other. When Udiya was five she brought him to the school. She wanted him to start learning. The school was just next door. My father was the Headmaster. Mushi's trust was in my father's cane—though he never used a cane on his students. Mushi was sure he could make a man of Udiya. Whenever I came home I was happy to see Mushi's dream taking shape. Udiya was doing well at school.

One year Mushi's husband came home for the raja festival and took Udiya away. The child, who was six, clung fiercely to his mother. She clung just as strongly to him. He had to be snatched away by force. That day Mushi looked utterly different, as though it was not Mushi but her ghost, a man-eating witch. At first she begged her husband, 'I have not neglected the child. We tend cows, but our Babu (my father) tends men. He will make a man of Udiya. Please don't take him away. How shall I live?' He did not say much in reply. How could he find the time? Wasn't he from Kolkata?

Bluntly he told her, 'The child is mine and I am taking him away. I married you only so that I could have a son—or else I wouldn't even have looked at you. Your father knew everything; it was all arranged with the matchmaker. I paid all the expenses of the wedding. Now don't create any trouble, or it will be bad for your son.'

Mushi's jaws clamped shut; her grip on her son loosened. She had no strength to hold on. Anything that might harm Udiya was like death to her. Udiya was howling, 'Mother, mother,' sobbing so hard that he was unable to draw breath. Her husband dragged him away ... He had taken Mushi's womb on hire briefly, so that his line might survive. He had made her a wife, then a mother—given her all that a woman could want. What more could she expect?

But is giving birth to a human being like share-cropping?— Sow your seed on another's land and when your crops have grown tall, carry them away to your own barn? Give the owner of the land just a whiff of the crops, that's all. For five years, Udiya had called Mushi 'Mother.' That was her share.

She lay in a heap on her bed, muttering to herself. The world of law courts was unknown to her. Where could she have found justice?

When the money orders from Kolkata ceased, Tinka's attitude changed completely. Somehow, Mushi dragged herself to work. Her old parents were receiving the same treatment that she was. She had to keep herself alive to look after them. But her thoughts were mainly of Udiya.

When I came home the next time I heard she was suffering from some incurable disease. The village physician had no idea what it was. Tinka could have taken her to the government hospital, but he was reluctant to spend money on her. I went to see Mushi. She looked at me with brimming eyes but said nothing. I said 'Don't you recognize me? Who am I?'

'Udiya,' she replied. Everyone she saw now was Udiya.

On my next visit I heard she was dead. It was not even a year since Udiya had left.

Today, after a very long time, I have remembered Mushi. I asked myself, how old could she have been when she died? On taking stock, the answer was 'six years'. She had lived only as long as she heard Udiya's call of 'Mother'.

—*Translated from the Oriya by Bikram Das*

Indira Goswami

I See the Yamuna on the Horizon

Today, I would like to shed this plain, white blouse, which has been clinging to my body for the last few days. Today, I would like to wear a bright green dress, widen the vermilion dot drawn in the centre of my broad forehead, sprinkle vermilion in the parting of my hair, like the straight veins of a sliced cucumber. So that people would realize, even at a distance of thirty feet, that I am married. A faithful, dutiful wife to my dear husband.

I sat down on the sofa, placed on one side of the veranda, a sofa on which we had spent many pleasant moments ... that is right, pleasant moments of our conjugal life. The cushions which bore my neat stitches, lay crumpled, their corners almost drooping. I buried my face in one of them and tried to imagine my husband's fingers running through my hair. I tried to remember if the familiar scent of my husband's chest could make me forget the world. I generally do not think of such things, nor do I wish to. But today, there is a reason for it.

Today my entire existence—my conscious and my subconscious being is filled with joy, because I am about to become a mother. I long to give the news to my husband. I feel as if after this I will be able to spend my days in deep contentment and inexplicable bliss. I will be able to chase away the sense of frustration that has been unfailingly shadowing me.

My father had held a government job in Shillong. I spent an uneventful childhood with Ma, Deuta and our old servant Manokai. Manokai was the vigilant sentry of my childhood, dropping me to school and picking me up, keeping an eye on my meals, trailing me like a shadow. I have a faint memory of the road in front of my house in winter, swept with dry leaves. Leaves that were as slippery and smooth as a young woman's shampooed tresses. I remember too the village, full of wild roses that had no smell. Grasping Manokai's hand, I would often ask him a question: 'Look, Manokai, don't those bald hills look like weary camels sitting down to rest?' With Manokai around, I could not stand the company of children of my age for long, a habit my parents discussed openly. I noticed Deuta look slightly worried, but a contended smile hovered on Ma's lips.

I remember, below our compound was a row of straw huts. I had noticed for a long time, huge locks dangling on two doors at the end of the row. One day, from our terrace, I saw that the doors were open. A coconut rope was strung between a pillar on the veranda and the peach tree in front. Two small frocks, a pair of pyjamas and a 'chadar' hung there. My gaze slid to the other end of the veranda, where a girl of my age was lost in her game of bride-and-groom. Playing with rags and broken tins, she was talking to herself so enthusiastically that I wanted to play with her, to be like her. I remember very well, I had experienced a child-like greed for her company. That was the first time I had felt like playing with somebody of my age.

After that, whenever I could shake off Ma and Manokai, I would climb on the terrace, stare unblinkingly at the straw hut, probably gaze with a child's all-consuming curiosity at the little girl wrapped in her solitary game.

I remember—one day after coming back from school, I was

standing on the veranda, drinking a glass of milk when I started as though I had seen something peculiar. The little girl from the last room in the row of straw huts was walking towards me, that is, she seemed to be coming my way. Lifting her eyes, round and bright like that of a gom snake's, she told me from a distance, 'Come, let us cross the gate and go and play near the bridge— the broken bridge near the stream.'

I had followed her, as if in a trance. As I climbed on a plank to push open the gate, which was too high for me, I had felt something grasp my arm. It was Manokai. On the steps in front of our house stood Ma, looking at me. The little girl darted away like a thief and I hid my face in Manokai's shirt. From that day, Manokai would take me to play with a group of children in 'Hydri' park.

When he took me for a walk past the straw huts, the little girl who lived in the last house would curl her lip and whisper, loud enough for me to hear, 'Ma says, you are a parrot in a cage. You can only repeat what people say.' I did not understand her words. When I asked Manokai, he said that those words had no meaning.

Gradually I forgot the little girl.

In the meantime, I passed out of school and took admission in college. I stacked my frocks away in a bamboo basket. I cut off the buttons which still looked new from those frocks and sewed them on my blouses. I noticed that Manokai no longer followed me like a shadow. A time came when he was careful about what he said to me. A few chores were added to my daily work. Every evening I had to light the lamp in the prayer room and read a few religious texts.

I read them, but what I liked better was the idea of saying a few words to myself, sitting in front of the still idol made of sandalwood. The woman in me would be inexplicably thrilled by the meaningless conversations I had with the lifeless idol. I believed that traditional faith had its power. Sometimes, of course, I could not help laughing at myself. But then I would pull the book towards me, for fear of invoking the curse of the gods.

Even then, sometimes, I would quietly steal away to the terrace with a novel I was embarrassed to read in front of Ma. Ma and Manokai no longer raised a hue and cry looking for me—my behaviour had convinced them that I was a harmless, scatterbrained girl.

One day, from the terrace, I saw the short, stout girl, dressed in a red-bordered sari, emerge from the last room in the row of straw huts and make for our house. I descended the stairs. She sat down on a *morha* in the veranda, as if she were an old acquaintance. Looking me in the eye, she said, 'You have put on weight, you have also become more grave. The light that danced in your eyes has now disappeared.'

I heard myself saying, 'You have become grave too—the mischief is no longer there.' Raising those eyes shaped like kund petals to me, she said, 'I am still mischievous in a different sense. In a way that allows me to enjoy myself ... enjoy quite a few things. Aimano, you would not understand these things. Do you remember, when I was a child, I called you a caged parrot?'

She pulled the plait swinging on her back to her left, twined the silk threads at the end of the tassel round her fingers and with her eyes dropping with shyness, said, 'I wanted to request you to do something, if you do not mind.'

I shook my head, 'No!'

'You will have to write a letter for me—a reply to this one.' Pulling a letter out of her blouse, she read it aloud to me. For some time I was mute, entranced. I had heard about love letters written with such passion in books, but this was the first time I had read a letter actually written by someone for his love.

'You are an educated girl, please write a nice reply to this.'

I protested, but to no avail. She was so persistent that I was finally forced to concede. Before she left, she whispered in my ears, 'I am going to trouble you for a few more days ... Please do not mind.'

For several days after that I wrote letters for Sunanda, into which I poured my heart and which were drenched with my emotions. I wrote them with a distinct sense of contentment. Such was my involvement in the letters that I was scared Sunanda would suddenly spring the news of her wedding on me and deprive me of this bit of satisfaction.

But one day I woke up. Sunanda reminded me that my first love letter had been written on behalf of somebody. These were words which I should have spoken to somebody. I had gifted them to another young woman. A childlike smile curving her lips, Sunanda told me, 'When I read your letters I feel as if you are used to writing such things. Honestly, has nobody ever written to you?'

'No, nobody has written such letters to me,' I said, and then added harshly, 'They would not dare. And I would not have spared them.'

She said gently, 'There is no question of daring. When you have infinite love, you have strength and courage. Love is divine, not despicable.'

After this she came to me only for a few days. Then the visits stopped completely. The two of them had worked out their lives so beautifully that my role was not at all necessary.

Gradually I started to experience a sense of discontentment. I frequently remembered Sunanda's cunning gaze and her sharp words, 'You are beautiful, you have a body as succulent as the flesh of ripe bel fruit. Has nobody poured out his heart to you? Has nobody spoken two sentences to you, drenched with passion?' I was convinced that my beauty, my youth was like a picture without life, like dry wood! Nobody found me attractive.

A time came when I bickered with everybody in the house for no apparent reason. I roamed aimlessly along the lake with my cook for company. I blamed Ma, Manokai and the conservative environment of our house for my escapist thoughts—it occurred to me that from my childhood, my actions had been monitored by people surrounding me like vigilant sentries. All my attempts at self-expression had met with reprimands and humiliation.

Once, when I had arranged the flowers in the vase atop the dining table, Ma had told me—'Look, Aimano, white flowers would go better with these yellow ones, rather than blue sweet peas.' She had taken out the blue flowers and put others in their place.

That is not all. When, before an outing, I wore something of my choice, Ma would walk about me several times, looking me up and down with a critical eye. Finally, unable to control herself, she would say, 'Aimano, the sari folds do not look very good if you drape them on top of one another ... the blouse does not match the sari border ... do not comb your hair in that flat style if you want to plait it.'

I would obey her without question for I believed I did not know how to dress myself. When I did, I cut a ridiculous figure. I felt that my face wore a dumb look, which is why nobody was drawn to me.

Lying in bed at night, I was troubled by the same thoughts. I could not really blame anybody for this uneventful life of mine. And my ignorance about this linear existence had been a blessing.

But a very ordinary young woman had taught me that in this world I was not at all equipped to express myself. I was truly a parrot in a cage, everybody would tell me which way to go—in my childhood it was my parents, in my youth it would be my husband and in my old age, my children.

But most girls of upper classes lived their lives as aristocratic toys, and Ma would spare no opportunity to tell me that they were the repositories of actual happiness. That was the same measure of happiness that fate had in store for me.

But Sunanda had told me, 'Love brought in by the bonds of marriage is not true love. Love has to be spontaneous, there should no compulsions.'

No, I thought, I should not lay much store by these words. Most people were happy in this way. A few days passed. I became more composed. Finally, a day came when realization dawned on me.

*

One day I returned home from college to find Ma and Manokai sitting with very long faces. I saw that a small camp bed had been squeezed into my study. I understood that we were expecting a guest.

I faintly heard Ma and Manokai talking near the corridor. Ma's voice was harsh, 'I had forbidden it initially. Deuta has gone ahead and asked him over. I am not in favour of inviting young men home from all over the place ...'

Aideu, Deuta said, he was married. But there has been an accident recently.

I did not hear the rest of the words.

I looked at the room as if I was seeing it for the first time. Were there cobwebs in a corner of the windows? Were there evidence of my carelessness, had I scribbled poetry on the wall, near the table? No, I had not—thankfully, for if the man found out that I scribbled lines of poetry here and there he would conclude that I was a love-starved, frivolous young woman. Or that I was so deeply in love that I found poetry everywhere in the universe. How would he know that an ordinary young woman had taught me an extraordinary lesson? How would he know that I was deprived of love, spontaneous and empowering, encouraging aspirations to immortality? How would he understand that I had to force that love out of the man who married me?

In the meantime, my father returned from office. I got to hear again that this friend's son had been married, but had lost his wife in an accident.

I felt a strange tenderness for the man I was yet to meet.

Finally he arrived at the fall of dusk.

At the earliest opportunity I slipped into his room. His bed was neatly made, Manokai must have done it. The almirah stood in a corner, overflowing with white clothes. On the shelf lay a small oval mirror, his comb, toothbrush, other articles of daily use. I smelt a gentle, pleasant odour waft out of them.

Suddenly my eyes fell on a handkerchief lying at the foot of the table, somebody had put buttonhole stitches along its borders. I picked it up and fingered it. It must have been stitched by his wife. The stitches were neat, the lady must have been skilled. And she must have been beautiful, too, for people said that one required fingers, graceful and tapering like the petals of a banana flower, for good needlework. My eye fell on a white kurta on the almirah. A few buttons were missing from it. I felt a wave of sorrow sweep over me. He must have been thoroughly indulged, he could not even take care of his little needs.

At one point in the evening, the lights in the room came on. The man was sitting on a chair, reading a book. His face was partially visible to me—I could not tear my eyes away. I felt as if I had seen the man somewhere, those eyes, the lips, they were very familiar.

A time came when he sat about a foot away from me, sipping tea which I had poured out, a time came when I could raise my head to speak to him—I have not understood *Christabel* at all, it will only take half an hour. I could sit by his side, watering my plants, without any inhibitions. That was the first instance of my familiarity with a man who was not a member of my family.

A question rose in my mind. I battled with myself secretly. I would ask Krishendu, did you know your wife before you married her? Or was it a marriage fixed by your parents, the day you ushered her into your life, was it the day when you first met her?

The woman in me longed to ask him those questions.

The moments I spent inside Krishendu's room were steeped in a sense of unprecedented happiness, an ineffable excitement. My secret dreams would swirl around him. I thought of calling Sunanda over and pointing him out to her, 'This is the man.' No mortal joy could parallel the experience of my love for him.

But no ... softer emotions flowing through my mind submerged passionate sentiments. A thought stirred in me: I will lay claim to your love only if you have not exchanged it with your wife before your marriage, if only your love for her was not spontaneous but something you embraced out of compulsion.

*

Our Christmas holidays had started. These chilly December days were my favourites. I had always liked to sit near the fireplace, watching the detached beauty of the pines through the open window. The soothing notes of Christmas carols sung in the nearby Roman Catholic church swept my mind to remote snow-clad lands, their nooks and corners and landscapes.

I heard Krishendu's footsteps in the room adjacent to mine. I heard him cough a few times.

Reflected in my gaze, yet not admitted by my conscious mind, were words spoken by a simple young woman, untouched by the rays of education. She had indeed reminded me of the young woman hungry for love, trapped in a thick net of pride, of compassion for my parents, mingled with fear. That is why I could never search out a pair of eyes among surging crowds, a pair of eyes as bright as those of a mountain snake's on a dark night. A simple, unschooled young woman had alerted me about this mask of mine. It occurred to me that education could do nothing to this old, primitive hunger. Everything could be cultured expect for love.

In the next room, Krishendu coughed again. I tried to picture his wife—had she been here, what would she have been doing? She might have sat close to Krishendu, knitting a sweater. Her fingers would pick up speed in tandem with the cold wind outside, scattering her hair on her cheeks and forehead.

I suddenly remembered an incident. I still think about it often, and when I do, a strange, inexplicable excitement, mingled with a sense of shame, threatens to engulf me.

One day Krishendu had been unwell, he had a slight fever. When I saw his wan face, I decided that I would not go to college. Instead, I would sit by his bedside. Nobody would be able to make me leave his side.

I sat down by his bed. When his eye flickered open, my fingers were running through his hair. One of his feverish hands rose as if to touch my arm. I felt the heat sear my body. But when my gaze met his, the hand slid down because my look contained a simple thought, as uncomplicated as a child's. Like a drop of cold water.

After that incident Krishendu would have been awkward with me, but I did not give him a chance. Because I had gradually realized that it was my heart which sought Krishendu and not this corporeal body of mine.

The fireplace in Krishendu's room was not lit. He was huddled in a corner of his bed, buried in all the cold of a December evening. He eagerly accepted my invitation to sit in the warm drawing room.

We talked about trivial domestic matters. The old doubt started worrying me: did you know your wife before you married her? If so, for how long?

But no, I could not bring myself to ask him that question. I would not know how to direct my heart after hearing his answer.

'Would you like a cup of hot coffee?'

He nodded.

Sometime later, when I offered him the coffee, Krishendu asked me, 'What about you?'

'I do not feel like it.'

My heart spoke up: 'You could have poured half of yours on the plate. Do you know what I would have said if you had done so: have half the coffee and keep an equal share for me.'

I felt like putting a few pieces of coal in the fire. Let the smoke veil my face's pallor, my distracted look. We sat in silence for long time. Though we sat just a yard away from each other, we seemed to inhabit different worlds.

I saw Krishendu staring at the hand lying listlessly on my knee, a gaze misty in poetry, 'Come, put your hand in mine—tell me, why your heart weeps silently ...'

I pulled my chair away. I wrapped the 'chadar' closer around my body, so that not a single part would be visible to him, except for my fingers.

*

I got married. His work completed, Krishendu moved away.

I spared no efforts to lead my new life as lovingly and smoothly as possible. Sometimes of course, disturbing thoughts assailed me. My husband had married me to sire an heir and not because he had been overwhelmed by a powerful attraction for me.

But I felt differently when I put Krishendu in his place. I

could have forced my parents to permit me to marry Krishendu. But I had no desire to share his bed, I could not imagine his physical being dissolving into mine. Krishendu inhabits my consciousness in a different form, which is not easy to communicate to the world through word or gesture.

I had once heard my parents talk about his wife. She was apparently a woman of stunning beauty. That is not all, she took life to be an unending melody. And Krishendu ... Krishendu had been deeply in love with his wife, even before he had married her. He had fallen out of favour with his family when he had married her.

How could I fulfil the unfulfilled hopes of that woman?

I visualized a limp, frail body, lying on a soft bed. A body trampled with disease to which Krishendu paid no heed. He must have ardently looked at the pair of eyes, which held all the light of the world.

Finally, I came to a decision. I told myself, in your barren heart, my love will always bloom. Like a wild flower concealed in the shade of a tree in a dense forest, my love will live and flourish, away from you.

I carefully combed my hair, so that all the strands were in place. In the crown of black hair, my parting stood out like a worn-out path between two forests on a moonlit night. I put vermilion in my hair, more than necessary. So that people realize, even at a distance of thirty feet, that I am married.

I opened my suitcase and took out a dress. My husband admired me immensely in it. I had never been particularly attentive to his likes, to what he liked me to wear for instance, or how he liked the rooms done up. But the advent of new life in my body seemed to have opened up a number of closed windows. My husband would make gentle fun of me, he would say that I was too sensitive for my age. Sometimes he would be irritated, but he would never openly question it.

Suddenly, I felt a surge of compassion for the man. I wanted to make him happy with all my heart.

I opened the window to the west of our bedroom. The moon had risen in the sky. It floated atop a scrap of cloud, the colour of mushroom. It looked like a veiled, smiling, old friend.

Looking at the unadulterated beauty, I thought to myself, may Krishendu bless me. Not me, but the newborn child. May it be a girl, contending with all the intricacies of life.

May her love be spontaneous. Let no one ever call her a caged parrot. Let her heart be uncluttered like a clear day. A girl who in the first flush of youth, would hear somebody say— I have escaped from harsh reality, from the cruel would. Shelter me in the shade of your love.

May I bear a girl, a girl who will never be tormented by the secret agonies of her mother.

Let it not be a boy, but a girl. Sober, dignified and happy.

—*Translated from the Ahomiya by Atreyi Gohain*

Vaidehi

A Memory Called Ammacchi

I could go on recounting Ammacchi's story. In several pages. But then to remember Ammacchi in detail can be a very exhausting experience. For those of you who know what this feels like, do I need to say more? To evoke memories of some people can be so tiring! Which is why I will relate whatever comes to my mind, without any stubborn fascination for particular incidents or for the manner in which they should be narrated. I will merely concentrate on being as brief as possible. And then I'll stop.

That day, wearing her hair parted to one side and in two plaits, Ammacchi had started for Shambhatta's house for the Satyanarayana puja. It has taken me all these years to realize that Ammacchi's enthusiasm for the puja had been because she was going to Shambhatta's house. But let that be. And what did she do in Shambhatta's house? Nothing. She would sit in a corner and gaze with unblinking concentration at everything and everyone. As if watching all the pomp that accompanied a mere Satyanarayana puja left her dumbstruck. As if no one knew that the real Ammacchi, far from being tongue-tied, could easily render others so. What if she never had a single paisa on her, ever.

It somehow seems unnecessary to talk of my relationship with Ammacchi or how we came to be friends. I was probably charmed by the force with which she spoke. Assertive Ammacchi! Everyone was afraid of her, she had no friends of her age. Girls were sure to be rebuked at home if they were spotted in Ammacchi's company. But then, it was perhaps Ammacchi's bold frankness that attracted me to her. Luckily, no one in my family objected to my being friends with her, and so it was that Ammacchi came to be my 'senior friend'. Of course, I had to hop four steps for every four she walked to keep up or to just walk hand-in-hand with her. And, though I did not completely understand what Ammacchi said, I was always there to say 'Yes, yes,' or to share a laugh or just to say, 'Let it be.'

So, that day Ammacchi went to the Satyanarayana puja. Venkappayya accosted her on the way. 'What is this? Like a Bombay lady. The hair parted on one side. Chhi, chhi, go home and comb your hair properly,' he said.

'You go home,' Ammacchi retorted. 'Go have your tea. Ask Amma, she will make it for you. Don't you interfere in my affairs. Baldhead! Don't shout at me just because you cannot ever have a parting-line on your head.' She grabbed my arm and said, 'Come on, walk fast or we will have to bump into every son of a dog.' Dragging me along, she cursed under her breath, 'Burnt-face! God knows where he came from to torment me like this.'

Those who dismissed Ammacchi as a law unto herself just could not understand her logic. Why shouldn't she change her hairstyle if Venkappayya disapproved of it, they would ask.

*

Ammacchi was the only child of Seetatte, who had no one else to call her own. It seems Ammacchi was barely six months old when her father died and Venkappayya, who was himself just six years of age, had entered this family that was bereft of a male caretaker. He ran errands for Seetatte, and lived in the same house. As he grew older, he believed that he had a right over Ammacchi. 'Who will offer to marry your daughter? But don't worry about that! I'm here,' he would say to Seetatte.

Venkappayya had spread the word around that he was to marry Ammacchi. As for Ammacchi, she hated him more and more with every passing day. 'Even a bullock used for ploughing is better … the squint-eyed fellow,' she would say, greatly amused.

As a matter of fact, Venkappayya was not at all squint-eyed. Unfathomable as Ammacchi's comments were sometimes, I would nevertheless laugh. And when Ammacchi said, 'O baldheaded Venkappayya', the hilarity of the situation was compounded by the fact that it was all spoken in full view of his shining bald pate, in a way that everyone but he could hear it. So, how could I, who had heard and seen everything, keep myself from laughing? And, when the listener laughs over every remark, doesn't it encourage the speaker to dare more? We were a happy twosome, Ammacchi and I.

To get back to that day.

'Let's go into town,' Ammacchi said to me.

'Yes.'

'We will go to the temple from there.'

'All right.'

'From there … Amma, do you need anything for the house?' Ammacchi asked Seetatte.

'Even if I do, why should you bother? There is Venkappayya for that. You want an excuse to roam about the town, don't you?'

'Why? Why do you still depend on him? You needed to once, but now, am I not here?'

'Okay, my lady, go and get them,' said Seetatte, giving Ammacchi a long list. What luck, Seetatte had conceded so readily.

Ammacchi was elated. 'Let's hurry,' she said. 'If that silly man comes in now, he will upset our plans.' She ran into the inner room and hurriedly undid her plaits to comb her hair. This time, she did not wear it in plaits, but let it fall after securing it at the nape of her neck. And when her hair bobbed up and down, Ammacchi asked enthusiastically, 'How do I look? Does it suit me?' Holding the Himalayan Bouquet powder box upside down, she vigorously tapped the bottom to force out the remnants into her small powder holder. One powder box would last Ammacchi a whole year. 'Amma doesn't use powder anymore. Actually, if she did, nothing wrong would happen. At the most, she would leave behind a faint fragrance whenever she walked past. But she is afraid of tongues wagging. People can put up with obnoxious smells, but never with fragrance. I could happily wring all their necks,' fulminated Ammacchi, as she energetically patted some powder on her face and rubbed at the blotches to even them out. She then powdered my face too, and put a red sandalpaste mark on my forehead. This is how it was whenever Ammacchi had to go out—she became celebration personified. But, *where* were we going?

'After Appa died, there has been nobody to enquire after us. Neither from his side nor from Amma's ... What would have happened to us if it had not been for Bappanadu jatre?' laughed Ammacchi. 'It's because we did not have anybody that Venkappayya could exploit the situation. Why doesn't he die?' she grumbled. Carefully arranging the pallu into three folds, she asked, 'Do you know how to fix the folds? You have to pin it slightly at the back. Come, let's see you do it.' I held the pallu against her shoulder and fastened it to the blouse. 'That's right,' she said. 'You are my only friend. Where would I be without you?' That is how Ammacchi was—even she was happy with what she had, she worried about what it would be like if she didn't have it. And, when she smiled, an expression of vivaciousness would spread across her features. Her laughter was very infectious.

Ammacchi. Ammacchi ...

Looking into a small, round mirror, carefully scrutinizing herself from all sides, she said, 'Do you know, there is a long, full-length mirror in Shambhatta's house? Where do you think it is? In Mai's room. You can see yourself from head to toe. How grand for Mai!'

'Why is it grand?'

'You have to grow up to know what I mean. Tell me, why does Mai need that mirror? What is there anyway for Mai to look at and from head to toe? If only I had the mirror.'

At last, the elaborate preparations were over. We were about to leave. Just then Venkappayya walked in.

'Venkappayya's kola is here!' Ammacchi's face seemed to fall, so I said, 'This fellow is not Venkappayya, but Kunkappayya.' Ammacchi fell to laughing uncontrollably. 'You are incomparable! Could anyone else have thought of him as Kunkappayya?' For a long time after that, I laboured under the delusion that Kunkappayya meant something very significant.

Ah, yes ... Venkappayya had walked in. 'What is it now?' he demanded. 'Where are you off to, parading yourself like this?'

'To Tokara Gudde,' said Ammacchi cheekily.

'Why do you need to go out?'

'To buy some poison. Now, make way.'

Barring our exit, Venkappayya began to scold Ammacchi. 'So, a pleated pallu. Like those town-women. Going out without even covering your breasts properly. Whose reputation do you want to destroy?' Venkappayya's outburst was aimed at Ammacchi, of course, but it was obvious that he was targeting me too.

Ammacchi glared at Venkappayya before she dismissed him with, 'Even if you go about in just a langoti, I wouldn't stop to question you. Why does it bother you when I do things the way I like doing them?'

'Go inside,' ordered Venkappayya.

'Who are you to order me around?' demanded Ammacchi.

'I'll break your limbs.'

'And you think I'll be sitting around munching groundnuts when you do that?' asked Ammacchi.

Venkappayya called out to Seetatte. 'Is it necessary for her to be going around town dressed like this? If you need anything won't I get them for you?' and then he played his trump card. 'Don't you realize, all this is only an excuse to go to Shambhatta's house? She is always going there. To laugh there, with her mouth wide open. They are sure to have counted the number of teeth in her mouth.'

My cries of 'All lies! Seetatte' fell on deaf ears.

Seetatte was ready with her 'Is it true girl?'

Ammacchi only said, 'If I am going to Shambhatta's house, I will tell you so, I have never felt the need to lie. Why do you listen to this Birkanakatte bhoota and shout at me?'

Seetatte lost her temper. 'Aiyo, don't argue, you hussy, don't say anything more. If we did not have Venkappayya to support us, then you'd know our plight ...' She almost pushed Ammacchi, who was standing outside by now, right back into the house.

Venkappayya looked at me as if he would swallow me up. I ran inside and hugged Ammacchi in great fright. Disengaging my arm, Ammacchi began to stroke my head. 'Don't be afraid. He is only a fake. Don't you be afraid of fakes. Come, let us weave thatches.' Ammacchi's voice quivered, but there was not the slightest trace of tears in her eyes. Ammacchi moved towards the coconut frond like an iceberg. Picking up a well-soaked coconut frond, she spread it in the courtyard. She also gave me a small frond, 'I will teach you to weave thatches. You should learn every skill. Don't accept defeat in anything.' Her constricted voice began to relax and, like a person who refuses to be overcome and who believes that she should always confront the present, Ammacchi continued to talk.

'Here, twist the leaf this way. Then bend it backwards. Twist every alternate leaf and join them one after the other. Secure it tight so that there are no gaps. This is how even mats are woven. I like weaving thatches.' She guided me—'This way.' Or hailed my efforts, saying, 'Shabash. From now on we shall weave three to four thatches everyday. Let's have a bet on who can weave more.' And then, 'Didn't realize how much time had passed. Is yours over? Join the edges and tie them into knots. That's it … I'll teach him a lesson. He was hoping I would cry. But would I cry so easily? If I don't drive him to tears, I'm not Ammacchi. Just let him wait till I get a husband and then he's had it.' Biting her lip, she went on twisting the ends of the thatch. 'Look how very broad it is! Broader than the mat we sit on. If we can weave like this everyday, we could use these to thatch out marriage pandals too!' she said, laughing. The corner of her eye shone. Whether in laughter, sorrow or anger, Ammacchi's eyes always burned bright.

*

'Amma, we are going to the temple!'

Ammacchi took me to Rama Teacher's house instead, explaining, 'So what? The world does not belong to people who speak the truth.' As if she knew I was surprised, she said, 'When I am not allowed to step out of the house, all because I spoke the truth, I have to resort to lying.'

Rama Teacher was a tailor. Ammacchi had taken a fancy to a back-buttoned blouse that she had seen the city girls at Shambhatta's house wear.

'Have you seen them?' she asked.

'No,' I replied.

'You never notice all that. It seems Rama Teacher stitches back-buttoned blouses very well. By the way, will you help me with the buttons till I get used to fastening them on my own?'

'Yes, I'll do them all.'

'But you won't tell anybody, will you?'

'No,' I promised.

Rama Teacher looked up from her sewing machine, lifting her eyebrows just a little, and then returned her gaze to the piece of cloth on her sewing machine. Bringing the machine to a halt, she held the thread up taut and bit it.

Ammacchi gave her the blouse-piece, saying, 'Make it a back-buttoned blouse, teacher, Amma need not know. I will take care of that.' That is Ammacchi: outside her house, she spoke 'Karnataka,' standard Kannada. Konkani-speaking Rama Teacher spoke this same polished accented Kannada.

While Ammacchi was getting measured for a back-buttoned blouse, it became clear that Rama Teacher was laughing constantly to herself, as if she had just heard a joke, I could not understand why. If Ammacchi fancied a back-buttoned blouse, why should that amuse Rama Teacher so?

Rama Teacher said to Ammacchi, 'I can make a back-buttoned blouse. It's not difficult. But, what if Venkappayya creates a scene? He obviously doesn't approve of all this.'

Rama Teacher knew everybody in the village, and every household and its internal affairs. And everyone knew Rama Teacher. But then, was Ammacchi the kind to be deterred by that?

'Hmm, what did you say, teacher? Is he the village headman to come here and make a scene? This is my blouse. Make it to my specifications,' Ammacchi said in a commanding tone. Rama Teacher seemed amused even at this. Ammacchi heaved a deep sigh and got up to leave.

On our way back, after a long spell of silence, Ammacchi

gave vent to her suppressed anger, 'What arrogance! Doesn't listen to me. Worried about what Venkappayya will say! Is the fellow my husband? I would much rather elope with any stranger than marry this fellow.'

And when she asked, 'What do you say?' I was there to say, 'Yes, of course.'

Shambhatta's house could be seen in the distance.

'Shall we go there now?' asked Ammacchi. 'There is still time before sunset.' But she changed her mind. 'No, not now ... that snake might be around somewhere and he will see us. They say Shambhatta's son is going to come back—now that his studies are over. It seems he will stay here, marry a village girl and take care of the fields. Isn't that good? But then, that mother of his—she is too proud! A termagant! They say she is capable of even beating up her husband! How could such a son be born to her? Have you seen him? We will go there once after he comes back. We'll cook up some story at home. He speaks so well and so much. Not like his mother who is so conceited ...'

And so we reached home that day.

*

Rama Teacher sent the tailored blouse home with Venkappayya. When Ammacchi went into her room to try the new blouse I saw Venkappayya look at Seetatte—who was pulling out the threads from dried banana stems and tying them into bundles—and smile. When it became clear to Venkappayya that I had noticed the smile, he looked at me as if I was a culprit, and saying, 'Must tell Malashmi Mai not to let her daughter in Ammacchi's company lest she turns out bad too,' he tried to scare me with his eyes. Just then I heard Ammacchi shriek. And I saw, in great astonishment, that Venkappayya and Seetatte were laughing noiselessly.

'Ammacchii…'

Ammacchi came out from her room and, in a most nonchalant manner, asked me, 'What is it? What did you call me for?' She went and sat with Venkappayya and Seetatte and started pulling the threads from the banana stems and twisting them into bundles.

In a voice tinged with laughter Seetatte asked, 'What? How does the blouse fit?'

'First-class! After all, Rama Teacher stitched it!' said Ammacchi, as if that was a fitting reply to Venkappayya. Then looking in his direction, she bit a thread and spat it out as if it was some terrible thing that she wanted to get rid of.

*

For eight days Venkappayya was not at home. It seems he went to Tirupati once a year. 'How terrible for God who has to see the likes of Venkappayya every year,' Ammacchi would often say. 'God should curse that squint-eyed fellow: If you step into this village again you will be reduced to ashes or be changed into a pit-licking crow living on the Konkan coast. If God could do that, I would go to Tirupati every year—but then, God has no sense! He will bless even people like Venkappayya who profit despite all the dirty tricks they play on others.'

Ammacchi whispered to me that day, 'Let's go into the python's room and see what it has hidden there.'

The first thing we spotted was Venkappayya's shirt hanging from a wooden peg. 'Look at Venkappayya swinging both his arms and hanging from the peg,' laughed Ammacchi. Standing some distance away, as if the very touch of the shirt was repulsive to her, she stretched her arm and removed the shirt from the peg. 'Come on, get me a pair of scissors, some thread and a needle. Amma shouldn't know.'

It was three o'clock in the afternoon and Seetatte was having her afternoon nap. I quickly fetched all the things Ammacchi had asked for. She deftly cut up the back of the shirt. She sewed up the front end, dislodged the buttons and, placing them haphazardly, stitched them into the cut end of the shirt. 'That's it! It's ready, the buffoon's shirt, special for the Tirupati-returned,' she announced as she replaced the shirt on the wooden peg. 'Did he suppose he could get away after conniving with Rama Teacher?' And turning to me, she said, 'Don't you tell Amma about this. If she learns of it on her own, let her, I'm not afraid of that.' I swore I would not tell Seetatte about it.

*

Venkappayya returned from Tirupati. Haa! Hou! Ho! he climbed the stairs, announcing his arrival. He began to describe the Tirupati vadas, laddus and curd-rice to us, quite oblivious of thoughts that were crossing Ammacchi's mind just then, who must have been inwardly mocking him—'Baldhead doesn't have to worry about offering his hair to God.'

Venkappayya announced his plans to open a hotel in Tirupati.

'Oh, that far!' said Seetatte.

Venkappayya elaborated his grand plans. 'If I open a hotel it will be far away from here. I will return to the village only after making money,' he said in the manner of a man of great common sense.

'At last we will be rid of this rare treasure,' said Ammacchi. Handing the prasada to Seetatte, Venkappayya said, 'Have it all of you.' And then, looking at Ammacchi, he said, 'It might straighten you out,' and went to have his bath.

Soon he came out saying, 'Now to eat, eat, eat. I'm ravenous. But I'll wear my shirt before that.' And he went to his room. It was Ravana who came out from the room. 'Where is that slut, the hussy ... what arrogance! I will ruin her.' Panic-stricken at the sound of Venkappayya's voice, I had huddled up against a corner on the stairs from where he picked me up as if I were a mouse, and demanded, 'Where is she? Tell me. Tell me. Or should I whack you?

Unmindful of Seetatte's alarmed queries, 'What is it, what happened? What is it now, what did the whore do this time?' Venkappayya went on tightening his grip on me and bellowing, 'Come on, tell me, where is ...'

'Ammacchiiiii ...' I shrieked.

Ammacchi came out and, leaning against the window, stood laughing. 'What,' she asked, 'after going to Tirupati, have your eyes become strange? I've been here all the while—can't you see? Why do you torture the child?' Venkappayya dropped me with a thud and growled, 'What did you say, what did you say?' he advanced towards Ammacchi, caught her by the hair and dragged her into his room and shut the door.

'Aiyo, aiyo! What is all this I can't bear to see it. Venkappayya. Venkappayya. Open the door ... Aiyo, the shrew ...' wailed Seetatte as if her very heart would break.

A while later, the door opened. Ammacchi came out. Her face was aflame. Blood was oozing from her lip.

'Ammacchi ... blood!'

My terrified shout did not evoke any reaction from Ammacchi, who was heading, very slowly, towards the inner room. And then, she turned to look at Seetatte and spat out the words, 'Die. Why are you alive? To kill me?' before she closed the door behind her.

Venkappayya remained sitting inside against a pillar, as if dead.

'Seetatte.'

In a voice full of pain, Seetatte said, 'Go child. Go home. Don't tell anybody what you saw here. You won't, will you?'

I promised Seetatte not to say anything to anyone.

Although, I did not breathe a word to anyone, the entire village knew about it the next day! How did that happen? My surprise knew no bounds. When people had tried in various ways to get something out of me, I pretended such innocence! They say children are incapable of pretence. Come to think of it, we all pretend best as children.

Now let me tell you what followed. Ammacchi and Venkappayya were married. Venkappayya opened his hotel, in Tirupati. Ammacchi went away with him.

'If I am alive, I will see you again. Don't be upset. Go to school, study hard and become smart. You should grow into an educated, cultured girl. Okay?' she said, caressing my hair, and then she walked away as if everything was over.

Even I had believed that everything was over.

*

School. Home. Between the two, one doesn't realize the number of days that pass. Then one day, whom do I see but Ammacchi— in the distance!

Ammacchi, Ammacchi! I jumped up from the window and ran. I took the handbag from her.

Holding the trunk in her hand, walking ahead of me, she talked breathlessly of the buses, trains, Tirupati, the deity's hand, the naamam on his forehead, their hotel, dosas, puris, idlis, vadas all in her characteristically nonchalant voice, as if nothing else had happened.

I had something to tell her, too. In a voice full of enthusiasm, I said, 'Ammachhi, Shambhatta's son, Sesha is here. It's four days now since he came. He is going to stay here now, Mai says.'

Ammacchi stooped, and turned to look at me as if trying to recall what she had just heard. Her eyes fixed on me, she said,

'Let them die, every one of them. Let everyone eat mud.'

Noticing that I was staring at her—lost, unable to understand her words—Ammacchi hugged me and said, 'Let everyone die. Except the two of us. I will talk and you'll laugh. Yes?'

But looking at Ammacchi, who resembled a piece of sculpted stone as she said this, who could laugh?

Finally we reached home. Having caught sight of Ammacchi in the distance, Seetatte was standing at the doorway, her hands supporting her back, completely dumbfounded. But, as soon as we reached the house, she demanded angrily, 'What, have you come alone, you whore? What did you do *this* time?'

'What else was I to do except come alone?' Ammacchi said. 'Your Venkappayya hanged himself.'

Ammacchi walked to the water-trough. She splashed water on her arms and feet before she turned to look at her mother's face. And then, wiping the water from her face with the pallu of her sari, she looked at me from the corner of her eye.

For some reason, I turned to look at Seetatte, who was screaming invectives by now. But strangely, her eyes did not reflect the anger that issued from her lips!

I remember those eyes to this day. Did they convey anything, I often wonder. But whatever it is that I remember today, because it conforms with what I desire to remember, I stop myself from looking further into those eyes. The only memory that lingers in my mind is the expression in Ammacchi's eyes as she wiped her face with her pallu—she was laughing from the corner of her eye.

—*Translated from the Kannada by Pranava Manjari N.*

Ismat Chughtai

The Quilt

In winter, when I put a quilt over myself, its shadows on the wall seem to sway like an elephant. That sends my mind racing into the labyrinth of times past. Memories come crowding in.

Sorry. I'm not going to regale you with a romantic tale about my quilt. It's hardly a subject for romance. It seems to me that the blanket, though less comfortable, does not cast shadows as terrifying as the quilt dancing on the wall.

I was then a small girl and fought all day with my brothers and their friends. Often I wondered why the hell I was so aggressive. At my age, my other sisters were busy drawing admirers, while I fought with any boy or girl I ran into.

That was why, when my mother went to Agra for about a week, she left me with an adopted sister of hers. She knew that there was no one in that house, not even a mouse, with whom I could get into a fight. It was a severe punishment for me! Amma left me with Begum Jaan, the same lady whose quilt is etched in my memory like the scar left by a blacksmith's brand. Her poor parents had agreed to marry her off to the nawab who was of 'ripe years' because he was very virtuous. No one had ever seen a nautch girl or prostitute in his house. He had performed hajj and helped several others undertake the holy pilgrimage.

He, however, had a strange hobby. Some people are crazy

enough to cultivate interests like breeding pigeons or watching cockfights. Nawab Saheb had only contempt for such disgusting sports. He kept an open house for students—young, fair slender-waisted boys whose expenses were borne by him.

Having married Begum Jaan, he tucked her away in the house with his other possessions and promptly forgot her. The frail, beautiful Begum wasted away in anguished loneliness.

One did not know when Begum Jaan's life began—whether it was when she committed the mistake of being born or when she came to the Nawab's house as his bride, climbed the four-poster bed and started counting her days. Or was it when she watched through the drawing-room door the increasing number of firm-calved, supple-waisted boys and the delicacies that were sent for them from the kitchen! Begum Jaan would have glimpses of them in their perfumed, flimsy shirts and feel as though she was being hauled over burning embers!

Or did it start when she gave up on amulets, talismans, black magic and other ways of retaining the love of her straying husband? She arranged for night-long readings from the Quran, but in vain. One cannot draw blood from a stone. The nawab didn't budge an inch. Begum Jaan was heartbroken and turned to books. But she found no relief. Romantic novels and sentimental verse depressed her even more. She began to spend sleepless nights, yearning for a love that had never been.

She felt like throwing all her clothes into the fire. One dressed up to impress people. But the nawab didn't have a moment to spare for her. He was too busy chasing the gossamer shirts. Nor did he allow her to go out. Relatives, however, would come for visits and stay on for months while she remained a prisoner in the house. These relatives, freeloaders all, made her blood boil. They helped themselves to rich food and got warm clothes made for themselves while she stiffened with cold despite the new cotton stuffed in her quilt. As she tossed and turned, her quilt

Ismat Chughtai

made newer shapes on the wall, but none of them held any promise of life for her. Then why must one live? Particularly, such a life as hers ... But then, Begum Jaan started living, and lived her life to the full.

It was Rabbu who rescued her from the fall.

Soon her thin body began to fill out. Her cheeks began to glow, and she blossomed. It was a special oil massage that brought life back to the half-dead Begum Jaan. Sorry, you won't find the recipe for this oil even in the most exclusive magazines.

When I first saw Begum Jaan, she was around forty. Reclining on the couch, she looked a picture of grandeur. Rabbu sat behind her, massaging her waist. A purple shawl covered her feet as she sat in regal splendour, a veritable maharani. I was fascinated by her looks and felt like sitting by her for hours, just adoring her. Her complexion was marble white, without a speck of ruddiness. Her hair was black and always bathed in oil. I had never seen the parting of her hair crooked, nor a single hair out of place. Her eyes were black and the elegantly plucked eyebrows seemed like two bows spread over the demure eyes. Her eyelids were heavy and her eyelashes dense. The most fascinating feature of her face, however, was her lips—usually coloured with lipstick and with a mere trace of down on her upper lips. Long hair covered her temples. Sometimes her face seemed to change shape under my gaze and looked as though it were the face of a young boy ...

Her skin was white and smooth, as though it had been stitched tightly over her body. When she stretched her legs for the massage, I stole a glance, enraptured by their sheen. She was very tall and the ample flesh on her body made her look stately and magnificent. Her hands were large and smooth, her waist exquisitely formed. Rabbu used to massage her back for hours together. It was as though the massage was one of the basic necessities of life. Rather, more important than life's necessities.

Rabbu had no other household duties. Perched on the couch she was always massaging some part or the other of Begum Jaan's body. At times I could hardly bear it—the sight of Rabbu massaging or rubbing at all hours. Speaking for myself, if anyone were to touch my body so often, I would certainly rot to death.

But even this daily massage wasn't enough. On the days when Begum Jaan took a bath, Rabbu would massage her body with a variety of oils and pastes for two hours. And she would massage with such vigour that even imagining it made me sick. The doors would be closed, the braziers would be lit, and then the session would begin. Usually Rabbu was the only person allowed to remain inside on such occasions. Other maids handed over the necessary things at the door, muttering disapproval.

In fact, Begum Jaan was afflicted with a persistent itch. Despite the oils and balms, the stubborn itch remained. Doctors and hakeems pronounced that nothing was wrong, the skin was unblemished. It could be an infection under the skin. 'These doctors are crazy ... There's nothing wrong with you,' Rabbu would say, smiling while she gazed at Begum Jaan dreamily.

Rabbu. She was as dark as Begum Jaan was fair, as purple as the other was white. She seemed to glow like heated iron. Her face was scarred by smallpox. She was short, stocky and had a small paunch. Her hands were small but agile, and her large, swollen lips were always wet. A strange sickening stench exuded from her body. And her tiny, puffy hands moved dexterously over Begum Jaan's body—now at her waist, now at her thighs, and now dashing to her ankles. Whenever I sat by Begum Jaan, my eyes would remain glued to those roving hands.

All through the year Begum Jaan wore white and billowing Hyderabadi jaali karga kurtas and brightly coloured pyjamas. And even when it was warm and the fan was on, she would cover herself with a light shawl. She loved winter. I too liked to be in her house in that season. She rarely moved out. Lying on the carpet she would munch dry fruits as Rabbu rubbed her back. The other maids were jealous of Rabbu. The witch! She ate, sat and even slept with Begum Jaan! Rabbu and Begum Jaan were the subject of their gossip during leisure hours. Someone would mention their names, and the whole group would burst into loud guffaws. What juicy stories they made up about them! Begum Jaan was oblivious to all this, cut off as she was from the world outside. Her existence was centred on herself and her itch.

I have already mentioned that I was very young at that time and was in love with Begum Jaan. She, too, was fond of me. When Amma decided to go to Agra, she left me with Begum Jaan for a week. She knew that if left alone at home I would fight with my brothers or roam around. The arrangement pleased both Begum Jaan and me. After all, she was Amma's adopted sister. Now the question was … where would I sleep? In Begum Jaan's room, naturally. A small bed was placed alongside hers. Till ten or eleven at night, we chatted and played 'Chance'. Then I went to bed. Rabbu was still rubbing her back as I fell asleep. 'Ugly woman!' I thought to myself.

I woke up at night and was scared. It was pitch dark and Begum Jaan's quilt was shaking vigorously, as though an elephant was struggling inside.

'Begum Jaan …' I could barely form the words out of fear. The elephant stopped shaking, and the quilt came down.

'What is it? Get back to sleep.' Begum Jaan's voice seemed to come from somewhere else.

'I'm scared,' I whimpered.

'Get back to sleep. What's there to be scared of? Recite the *Ayatul Kursi*.'

'All right …' I began to recite the prayer, but each time I reached 'ya lamu ma bain …' I forgot the lines though I knew the entire Ayat by heart.

'May I come to you, Begum Jaan?'

'No, child ... Get back to sleep.' Her tone was rather abrupt. Then I heard two people whispering. Oh God, who was this other person? I was really afraid.

'Begum Jaan ... I think a thief has entered the room.'

'Go back to sleep, child ... There's no thief.'

This was Rabbu's voice. I drew the quilt over my face and fell asleep.

By morning I had totally forgotten the terrifying scene enacted at night. I have always been superstitious—night fears, sleepwalking and talking in my sleep were daily occurrences in my childhood. Everyone used to say that I was possessed by evil spirits. So the incident slipped from my memory. The quilt looked perfectly innocent in the morning.

But the following night I woke up again and heard Begum Jaan and Rabbu arguing in subdued tones. I could not hear what the upshot of the tiff was, but I heard Rabbu crying. Then came the slurping sound of a cat licking a plate ... I was scared and went back to sleep.

The next day Rabbu went to see her son, an irascible young man. Begum Jaan had done a lot to help him out—bought him a shop, got him a job in the village. But nothing really pleased him. He stayed with Nawab Saheb for some time. The nawab got him new clothes and other gifts, but he ran away for no good reason and never came back, even to see Rabbu ...

Rabbu had gone to a relative's house to see her son. Begum Jaan was reluctant to let her go but realized that Rabbu was helpless. So she didn't prevent her from going.

All through the day Begum Jaan was out of sorts. Every joint ached, but she couldn't bear anyone's touch. She didn't eat anything and moped in bed all day.

'Shall I rub your back, Begum Jaan ...?' I asked zestfully as I shuffled the deck of cards. She peered at me.

'Shall I, really?' I put away the cards and began to rub her back while Begum Jaan lay there quietly.

Rabbu was due to return the next day ... but she didn't. Begum Jaan grew more and more irritable. She drank cup after cup of tea, and her head began to ache.

I resumed rubbing her back, which was smooth as the top of a table. I rubbed gently and was happy to be of some use to her.

'A little harder ... open the straps,' Begum Jaan said.

'Here ... a little below the shoulder ... that's right ... Ah! What pleasure ...' She expressed her satisfaction between sensuous breaths. 'A little further ...' Begum Jaan instructed though her hands could easily reach that spot. But she wanted me to stroke it. How proud I felt! 'Here ... oh, oh, you're tickling me ... Ah!' She smiled. I chatted away as I continued to massage her.

'I'll send you to the market tomorrow ... What do you want? ... A doll that sleeps and wakes up at your will?'

'No, Begum Jaan ... I don't want dolls ... Do you think I'm still a child?'

'So, you're an old woman then,' she laughed. 'If not a doll, I'll get you a babua ... Dress it up yourself. I'll give you a lot of old clothes. Okay?'

'Okay,' I answered.

'Here,' she would take my hand and place it where it itched and I, lost in the thought of the babua, kept scratching her listlessly while she talked.

'Listen ... you need some more frocks. I'll send for the tailor tomorrow and ask him to make new ones for you. Your mother has left some dress material.'

'I don't want that red material ... It looks so cheap.' I was chattering, oblivious of where my hands travelled. Begum Jaan lay still ... Oh God! I jerked my hand away.

'Hey girl, watch where your hands are ... You hurt my ribs.'
Begum Jaan smiled mischievously. I was embarrassed.

'Come here and lie down beside me ...' She made me lie
down with my head on her arm. 'How skinny you are ... your
ribs are showing.' She began counting my ribs.

I tried to protest.

'Come on, I'm not going to eat you up. How tight this
sweater is! And you don't have a warm vest on.' I felt very
uncomfortable.

'How many ribs does one have?' she changed the topic.

'Nine on one side, ten on the other,' I blurted out what I'd
learnt in school, rather incoherently.

'Take away your hand ... Let's see ... one, two, three ...'

I wanted to run away, but she held me tightly. I tried to
wriggle away, and Begum Jaan began to laugh loudly. To this
day, whenever I am reminded of her face at that moment, I feel
jittery. Her eyelids had dropped, her upper lip showed a black
shadow and tiny beads of sweat sparkled on her lips and nose
despite the cold. Her hands were as cold as ice but clammy as
though the skin had been stripped off. She wore a shawl, and in
the fine karga kurta, her body shone like a ball of dough. The
heavy gold buttons of the kurta were undone.

It was evening, and the room was getting enveloped in
darkness. A strange fear overcame me. Begum Jaan's deepset
eyes focussed on me and I felt like crying. She was pressing me
as though I were a clay doll and the odour of her warm body
made me want to throw up. But she was like a person possessed.
I could neither scream nor cry.

After some time she stopped and lay back exhausted. She
was breathing heavily, and her face looked pale and dull. I
thought she was going to die and rushed out of the room ...

Thank God Rabbu returned that night. Scared, I went to
bed rather early and pulled the quilt over me. But sleep evaded

me for hours.

Amma was taking so long to return from Agra! I was so terrified of Begum Jaan that I spent the whole day in the company of the maids. I felt too nervous to step into her room. What could I have said to anyone? That I was afraid of Begum Jaan? Begum Jaan who was so attached to me?

That day, Rabbu and Begum Jaan had another tiff. This did not augur well for me because Begum Jaan's thoughts were immediately directed towards me. She realized that I was wandering outdoors in the cold and might die of pneumonia. 'Child, do you want to put me to shame in public? If something happened to you, it would be a disaster.' She made me sit beside her as she washed her face and hands in the basin. Tea was set on a tripod next to her.

'Make tea, please ... and give me a cup,' she said as she wiped her face with a towel. 'I'll change in the meantime.'

I drank tea while she dressed. During her body massage she sent for me repeatedly. I went in, keeping my face turned away, and ran out after doing the errand. When she changed her dress I began to feel jittery. Turning my face away from her I sipped my tea.

My heart yearned in anguish for Amma. This punishment was much more severe than I deserved for fighting with my brothers. Amma always disliked my playing with boys. Now tell me, were they man-eaters that they would eat up her darling? And who were the boys? My own brothers and their puny little friends! She was a believer in strict segregation for women. But Begum Jaan here was more terrifying than all the loafers of the world. Left to myself, I would have run out into the street— even further away! But I was helpless and had to stay there much against my wish.

Begum Jaan had decked herself up elaborately and perfumed herself with the warm scent of attar. Then she began to shower me with affection. 'I want to go home,' was my answer to all her suggestions. Then I started crying.

'There, there ... come near me ... I'll take you to the market today. Okay?'

But I kept up the refrain of wanting to go home. All the toys and sweets of the world held no interest for me.

'Your brothers will bash you up, you witch.' She tapped me affectionately on my cheek.

'Let them.'

'Raw mangoes are sour to the taste, Begum Jaan,' hissed Rabbu, burning with jealousy.

Then, Begum Jaan had a fit. The gold necklace she had offered me moments ago was flung to the ground. The muslin net dupatta was torn to shreds. And her hair-parting which was never crooked, became a tangled mess.

'Oh! Oh! Oh!' she screamed between spasms. I ran out.

Begum Jaan regained her senses after a great deal of fuss and ministrations. When I peered into the room on tiptoe, I saw Rabbu rubbing her body, nestling against her waist.

'Take off your shoes,' Rabbu said while stroking Begum Jaan's ribs. Mouse-like, I snuggled into my quilt.

There was that peculiar noise again. In the dark Begum Jaan's quilt was once again swaying like an elephant. 'Allah! Ah! ...' I moaned in a feeble voice. The elephant inside the quilt heaved up and then sat down. I was mute. The elephant started to sway again. I was scared stiff. But I had resolved to switch on the light that night, come what may. The elephant started shaking once again, and it seemed as though it was trying to squat. There was the sound of someone smacking her lips, as though savouring a tasty pickle. Now I understood! Begum Jaan had not eaten anything the whole day. And Rabbu, the witch, was a notorious glutton. She must be polishing off some goodies. Flaring my nostrils I inhaled deeply. There was only the scent of attar, sandalwood and henna, nothing else.

Once again the quilt started swinging. I tried to lie still, but the quilt began to assume such grotesque shapes that I was shaken. It seemed as though a large frog was inflating itself noisily and was about to leap on to me.

'Aa ... Ammi ...' I whimpered. No one paid any heed. The quilt crept into my brain and began to grow larger. I stretched my leg nervously to the other side of the bed, groped for the switch and turned the light on. The elephant somersaulted inside the quilt which deflated immediately. During the somersault, a corner of the quilt rose by almost a foot ...

Good God! I gasped and sank deeper into my bed.

—*Translated from the Urdu by M. Asaduddin*

Kamala Das

A Doll for Rukmani

It was the same old story. The stepfather raping the minor girl while her mother was out visiting her relatives. The fat woman called Ayee by the inmates of the house threw back her head and laughed aloud, displaying two rows of brown teeth resembling rusty nails. 'Anasuya, what did you expect from a bum like your Govind?' she asked the thin visitor who had brought her twelve-year-old daughter for sale. 'Anyway, let bygones be bygones. Stop worrying about this nice-looking girl of yours. She will be all right here. You will hardly recognize her after a couple of months. What she needs is good food. Look at my girls, Anasuya. Do you see any one of them looking unhealthy? I feed them eggs with their parathas in the morning.' The little girl looked around. There were seven young women seated on the floor and all of them did look healthy. But peeping out of a window was a frail girl who wore orange bangles on her thin wrists. She could not have been more than fifteen. Perhaps she will be my friend, thought the little girl.

'Rukmani, come closer to me,' said Ayee, drawing the child to her swollen bosom. 'Take leave of your poor mother. She has a long way to go, and it is already late. The postman is returning home ...'

'Any letter for me?' asked Ayee, and the postman, slowing his bike, smiled good-humouredly at her.

'I am always hoping to hear from my beloved son, that good-for-nothing fellow who ran away from home ten years ago,' said Ayee.

'You will hear from him,' said the visitor, wiping a reddened nose on the corner of her sari. 'Your heart is pure. God will not make you suffer long.'

The child Rukmani looked at her mother with dry eyes. She was not unhappy about leaving her home. The man who had moved into her home some months ago, after her father had disappeared, was a monster. He not only beat up her mother every night but squeezed her own little breasts, hurting her dreadfully when she was alone in the house. And, last week he had pierced her body until she bled all over the floor.

'You ought not to have sent away the good man I married you off to, Anasuya,' said Ayee. 'He was a steady fellow and he never drank. But you lusted for a younger one. Are you satisfied now?'

'Do not taunt me so Ayee,' pleaded Anasuya. 'I have been a sinner. But please look after my child. She is innocent.'

Anasuya rolled the dirty currency notes in a paper and tucked the roll into her waist. 'I would not have taken any money from you, Ayee,' she said, a sob rising in her throat, 'but we are practically starving at home. The baby is given nothing but tea and maybe a banana at noon.'

When she left the place and walked towards the bus stop, the child Rukmani watched her, leaning against the bars of the porch. Finally, when her mother resembled a tiny green spot and dissolved with the other colours in the distance, she turned back to look at her new mother. Ayee was kneading lime and tobacco in the palm of her left hand. The thin girl emerged from the interior and smiled at Rukmani, crinkling her eyes. She was wearing a blue skirt and a torn white blouse. The bangles on her wrists had a frosted look.

'Do you wish to have some of these?' asked the thin girl. 'They are nylon bangles, not plastic. Ayee bought them for me at the fair last month.'

'Sita, you must teach Rukmani the customs of this place,' said Ayee. 'She is two years younger than you.'

Sita held Rukmani by her waist. 'You can have my bangles,' she said, looking at the child's wrists. Then she gave a laugh. 'Oh, you are big-made, aren't you?' Sita asked Rukmani. Rukmani's hands were large compared to Sita's pale ones. She felt clumsy all of a sudden. 'Orange will not suit a dark skin,' said Rukmani. 'You are not dark,' said Ayee. 'You have been walking to your school in the hot sun and that is why you have such a tan. We shall make you fair skinned in a month's time.'

A dark woman lying curled up on the floor, got up and glared at the child. 'What is wrong in being dark?' she asked Ayee. 'I am dark, but every client asks for me ...'

Sita dragged Rukmani into the corridor of the house which was dark and had a steamy smell. Then she was taken to a hall where on reed-mats, some young women were sleeping. One of them was wearing only a short skirt which had slipped up to reveal the cheeks of her buttocks. Rukmani looked away in disgust. 'Oh this one, she is utterly shameless,' said Sita, throwing a towel over the sleeping woman's legs. 'She is Radha. She has a bad temper. So be careful when you deal with her.' Sita pointed to a mat in the corner of the hall. 'That is where I sleep in the day,' she said. 'You may share the mat with me.'

'I cannot sleep in the day,' said Rukmani.

Sita laughed loudly and held on to her stomach as though it was about to burst. 'You are a baby,' she said. 'You are so innocent. Do you think we can sleep at night in this house? We shall all be so busy entertaining the visitors.'

'Visitors at night?' asked Rukmani. 'Who will come at night?'

Sita could not control her laughter. 'Oho ho,' she laughed, 'you are too funny, you will make me piss in my skirt ...'

Rukmani kept her satchel of books on the mat meant for her and Sita. 'Men come to do things here,' said Sita.

'What things?' asked Rukmani. She was thinking of her stepfather and the pain she had experienced when he climbed her on the floor.

'You will find out soon enough,' said Sita. 'Obey them or else Ayee will starve you to death. Do whatever they want you to do. Men are real dogs.'

Then they tiptoed out into the corridor while a soft voice asked them from inside a room, 'Who is it?' 'It is me, Sita,' said the pale girl. 'Don't make too much noise,' chided the soft voice.

'That is Mirathai, the favourite of this house,' said Sita in a whisper. 'Ayee has given her a room all to herself. She is a beautiful woman. And she is a matriculate, not like the rest of the gang who are all uneducated. How far have you studied, Rukmani?'

'I am in the sixth standard,' said Rukmani.

'That is good enough,' said Sita. 'You must be able to read English, just a little?'

'Not English,' said Rukmani. 'English is tough. We started it only this year. I can read Marathi and Hindi.'

'Then you must read out a book a client left for me to read. It contains dirty pictures of naked men and women. I pretended that I was educated and so he gave that book to me.' Saying this, Sita laughed again.

'Why do you hold your stomach when you laugh?' asked Rukmani.

'When I laugh I get a queasy feeling inside my belly,' Sita said. 'I am not too well these days. I have even lost my appetite.'

From the porch, rose a strident voice in protest. 'No, no, that is not true, Lachmi,' it said. 'I will never speak against your girls. You are like a younger sister to me. Besides, what can I say against your girls? Everybody knows that you keep a disciplined house and that your girls are plump and healthy. The Inspector Saheb told me that your Mira resembled a filmstar who has become of late very famous. I cannot recollect the name. It is a lengthy fashionable name.'

Ayee spread out her fat legs and leaned against the wall. She chewed the tobacco pensively for a minute. 'Where did you meet the Inspector Saheb, Sindhuthai?' she asked the visitor. The old woman took a pinch of tobacco from Ayee's betel box and pretended not to hear. Ayee repeated the question. Sindhuthai knew what a loaded question it was. 'I met him at Koushalya's place yesterday,' said Sindhuthai.

'The ingrate,' shouted Ayee. 'Here I give him expensive gifts and every week his hafta of fifty rupees and all the girls free, and he has the audacity to go to my rival's house for his quota of fun. What is wrong with my children? Are Koushalya's girls as clean as mine? Filthy, five rupeewalis.'

'Don't get upset, younger sister,' said Sindhuthai.

'Inspector Saheb said he was tired of women. He wanted little girls.'

'We don't have little girls,' asked Ayee. 'What about Sita? Is she not lovely with her white skin and petite figure?'

'Sita is not cooperative any longer he said,' whispered the hag.

'Have you seen the child I have bought today?' asked Ayee. 'Rukmani, come here and let Sindhuthai see you.'

Sita pushed Rukmani into the porch. The old woman pinched the child's calves and stroked her posterior. 'Yes, she is firm and sweet,' said Sindhuthai. 'How much did you pay for her? She must have cost you a lot of money.'

Ayee whispered something into the old woman's ear. 'Oh she is our Anasuya's child,' Sindhuthai said, 'that is why she has such beautiful legs.'

Kamala Das

'Will you tell the Inspector Saheb that we have this little Goddess in our house?' asked Ayee.

'Yes, I shall do so this very evening,' said Sindhuthai. She took some betel from the brass box and turned to go. Her gnarled hands with their dirty talons frightened the little girl. When the hag was staring at her, she had felt that a woodpecker was pecking at her skin. 'What an odious creature,' she murmured to Sita.

'Yes,' said Sita, 'she is a scandalmonger. I hate her.'

*

All the street lights were on but the sky was still grey when Mirathai's client, the college student, walked in with a swagger, calling out imperiously, 'Mira, Mira.' Ayee was still in the bathroom having her legs massaged with mustard oil but she heard his voice and frowned. 'It is that talkative swain again,' she remarked to the girl who was at her feet. 'If he does not pay this time, I shall get the police to throw him out,' continued Ayee. 'Radha, has he been to you any time?'

'No,' said Radha, 'he wants only Mira. He behaves as if he is her husband. He talks to her half the night and even quarrels.'

'Half the night?' asked Ayee. 'Does he pay for such a long session?'

'Don't ask me,' said Radha. 'After all Mira is your pet. None can question her in this house. She has begun to be fastidious of late. She refused even the Inspector Saheb yesterday complaining that she had a headache. She does not behave like a prostitute. She wants to be faithful to her college student ...'

'Don't use such coarse terms, Radha,' said Ayee.

'You do not like the word *prostitute*,' muttered Radha, 'but you know well that all of us are prostitutes. I believe in being frank and truthful.'

'Rub my knee harder,' said Ayee.

From Mira's closed room rose the rumble of a male voice. Mira laughed once.

Ayee was disturbed. 'What is he always talking about?' asked Ayee.

'He is teaching her politics,' said Radha.

'He is impotent, is he?' asked Ayee.

'I do not know, Ayee,' said the girl. 'He does not touch any of us. All I know is that he leaves Mira always with a headache. After he has visited her, she refuses to entertain any client. She sits on her bed humming strange tunes.' Ayee got up and walked towards the closed door. The young man was still talking briskly and Ayee could only pick out certain words which were familiar. Once or twice, he mentioned the word 'revolution'. Ayee knocked on the door. 'Who is it?' asked Mira. 'Open the door,' said Ayee. Mira opened the door. She was wearing her green sari and on the bed which still had an uncrumpled sheet, sat the student, smoking.

'Do you come all the way here to tell her of a revolution?' asked Ayee.

The youth coloured. 'I have paid the money,' he said. Ayee looked at him with contempt. 'This is a brothel,' she said, 'not a conference hall. Get on with your job and get out,' added Ayee. 'Other clients will be coming in a few minutes' time.'

The door was shut again. Ayee went up to the porch and surveyed the scene. The girls were wearing clothes sparkling with jari and sequins. They had make-up on their faces and flowers in their hair. The two young ones were playing with bits of tiles on a large diagram chalked out on the floor. 'Stop this childish game, Sita,' ordered Ayee. 'The clients are about to arrive.'

At that precise moment, the Inspector who was a burly man entered the porch and pointing to Rukmani asked: 'Is this your new recruit?' Ayee nodded. 'Come in,' said the man dragging the child into the interior.

'Go child, he is our friend,' said Ayee.

The Inspector threw the child on a charpoy and lifted her frock. 'You wear underpants like girls of the upper classes,' said the man, laughing. Rukmani felt his hands on her and struggled to get free. 'Let me go,' she cried, 'if you don't, I shall scratch your eyes out.'

'What did you say, you wild cat?' asked the angry man. His voice underwent a change, and became very hoarse. 'You will scratch me, will you, little whore ...'

'I am not a whore,' cried Rukmani. But the man did not care to listen. He was panting as though he had run a race and there was froth at the corners of his wide mouth. Later, he turned over and closed his eyes. 'I shall buy you a red frock,' he whispered, 'and panties with lace on them.'

Rukmani rose from the bed and ran back to the porch. Her hair was tousled and sweat beaded her brow. But she began once again to hop in the squares of the diagram while Sita watched animatedly. 'I have won,' cried Rukmani a little while later in triumph. Just then, the Inspector came out of the room and gave Ayee a slow smile.

'She is a vixen, all right. Knows the tricks of the trade. I liked her immensely.'

Rukmani glanced at the man whose face was red with the scratches inflicted by her own nails. He looked complacent.

'Who is prattling away in Mira's room?' asked the Inspector.

Ayee beat her head in mock anguish: 'It is that student again, come to teach her politics.'

'I can drive him out this place,' said the Inspector, 'only give me a day's notice. I can even get him arrested and sent to jail.'

'I know you can,' said Ayee. 'But let us wait until Mira tires of him. Mira is like my daughter. I love her dearly. I don't wish to hurt her feelings.'

'You have spoilt her already, Lachmibai,' said the Inspector.

'She behaves as if she is well born.'

'Who can say for certain that she is not well-born?' asked Ayee. 'When I found her at my doorstep, she was wrapped in an expensive silk sari, not the kind worn by people of our station.'

'Her mother must have been a maid working for a rich woman who gave that sari to her for Diwali or some such function,' said the man, reaching for Ayee's betel box.

'She certainly does not look like a poor woman's child,' said Ayee. 'Whenever I take the girls out to the town for shopping, people stare at her with hungry eyes. If my lost son were to return, I shall certainly marry her off to him. They will make a fine couple. Both are fair skinned, and both have light eyes.'

'Is your son's father a Chitpavan Brahmin?' asked the Inspector and both he and the old woman laughed in mirth. 'I must get going,' said the man.

'Is it true that you have started to visit Koushalya's place?' asked Ayee. 'Do not leave my place without giving me a truthful answer.'

'I shall get that witch Sindhuthai arrested and sent to jail,' said the man. 'She must have seen me walk past that house yesterday towards the bus stop, and she did not waste time in passing the information to you. Why should I go to that house, Lachmibai?'

Ayee blew out her nose and looked as if she was about to cry. 'That Koushalya, she spreads such horrible tales about my innocent girls,' said Ayee. 'Sindhuthai said that she was telling people that my girls were diseased. What will happen to our business if such stories are circulated. My poor girls will starve to death.'

'Don't cry,' said the Inspector, sheepishly stroking the woman's plump hand. 'I shall protect your reputation. I am your friend. I shall never let you down.'

Ayee brightened up a little. She even attempted a smile. 'Take some paan, Inspector Saheb,' she whispered.

After the Inspector had left, Ayee slipped into a sullen mood. She began to taunt her girls who were looking out through the bars. 'What is wrong with all of you,' she asked, 'have you forgotten how to attract men? I waste my money buying eggs and dalda and fish for all of you but not one of you know how to hold onto a man except that Mira and now she has latched on to a good-for-nothing fellow who teaches her politics. How many important people pass this way in their cars, slowing down as they pass this way to be able to see you and yet you do not do a thing to lure them in. What a bunch of pigs I have reared here. Koushalya is far more fortunate than I am. She whips her girls but that has only done them good. Look at the cars that have stopped near her place. Two already and it is not yet eight o'clock. I am going to throw you all out and go to Benaras. Let me at least die in peace ...'

The dark girl called Saraswati climbed down the porch and gestured to a young man who was watching out from a bus. Within a few minutes the young man was at her side, having got off at the next bus stop. She took him into the corridor, swinging her full hips and walking ahead of him. Ayee rubbed her eyes with the edge of her sari.

'I don't do these things because it is crude,' said the girl called Radha. 'I hate to stand out and solicit like a common streetwalker.' Then someone came asking for Sita. 'Ayee, not tonight,' begged Sita, wanting to be let off.

'Go with him child,' said Ayee, pushing Sita gently beyond the doorway.

'Rukmani, do not remove my piece from that square,' cried Sita. 'I shall be back to finish the game. He is a kind man, although a Madrasi,' said Ayee. 'He is working in a school. Comes during the first week of every month and only selects

Sita. He has three grown-up daughters studying in college. His wife is stricken with Arthritis. He tells me all about his life. He does not hide anything. He is not secretive like the others ...'

Ayee heard the sound of a woman's weeping from inside the house. She listened in silence for a moment or two. 'Is that our Mira weeping?' she asked. 'Go and see what is happening inside her room. Men are odd creatures. One cannot predict their actions. When I was young, a rich man came to me and whipped me for half an hour and went his way paying me thirty rupees. In those days, thirty was a large sum of money. I was too astonished to cry. I used to wait for him but he never turned up again.'

'What was your son's father like, Ayee?' asked Radha.

Ayee got up and gave a friendly slap on her cheek. 'Don't you dare talk about the father of my son,' said Ayee. 'He was a Brahmin. He was not like any of the men who come here to see all of you. He was a wise man. He used to recite the scriptures while dressing up to go.'

'He sounds so much like our Mirathai's friend,' said Radha. 'He sings the *Gitagovinda* to her on some nights. I have heard her trying to sing the song that he has taught her.'

'Mira has a sweet voice,' said Ayee. 'She is a gem of a girl. I wonder who left her on my doorstep nineteen years ago? Perhaps it was some high-born woman who had conceived while her husband was away.'

'Perhaps it was some harlot who did not want to be saddled with a baby,' said Radha.

'All of you are jealous of Mira,' said Ayee.

Just then Mira's client walked out without looking back even once. Ayee sat up in surprise. He looked as if he had been weeping too. What was wrong with the young man? Was he mentally imbalanced? She decided to speak to Mira about him. It would not do to encourage such an eccentric. Mira ought to try and bait a man of substance, a businessman who is tired of his wife or a politician who craves for relaxation off and on, someone who can bring her expensive gifts and bestow on the house a certain prestige.

'Mira,' Ayee called out to the weeping girl, 'come out this minute.' Mira came out and stood under the neon lamp, moon-coloured and slender. Only her eyes made large by collyrium looked red. 'What has he done to you, my daughter?' asked Ayee.

'He did nothing, Ayee,' said Mira. 'He is always kind to me.'

'What made you weep?' asked the old woman. 'He must have said something to upset you.' Mira looked down at her feet. She did not reply.

'Did he call you names?' asked Ayee.

'No, Ayee,' said Mira, 'he said that he had to sell his pen to visit me. He has no income of his own. He comes here saving his lunch-allowance and his bus fare. He loves me ...' Mira's eyes filled with tears.

*

When Sita vomited all over the floor of the room and scared her client away, Ayee was very angry with her. The man had asked for a refund of the money he had paid Ayee and had as a parting shot exclaimed that the house was full of diseased whores. Ayee entered the room to find Sita seated on the floor with vomit all around her and making a loud sound while she struggled to bring out more from her stomach. Her eyes were wide with fear. Ayee pulled her by her long braid and slapped her hard on her face. 'You have ruined the reputation of this house,' said Ayee. 'You eat all kinds of dirty things sold by the street vendors and throw up into the faces of our clients. How many times have I told you never to eat pani-puri or bhel?

Ungrateful girl. I will see that you starve for three days.'

Sita began to weep: 'Ayee, it is not my fault,' she whimpered. 'I have not been feeling well for the past few days. I cannot eat anything. I feel a heart-burn in the evenings ...'

'You have lost some weight,' said Ayee. Then she lifted the girl's white blouse and pierced at her tiny breasts. 'It is not possible,' murmured Ayee. 'You have not even attained puberty.'

Sita was given three days' leave. She was overjoyed. 'I do not have to attend to any man for three days,' she cried out in a voice thickened with happiness. 'We shall play hopscotch with bits of tiles, Rukmani, for hours and hours.'

Leaning against the bars of the porch, Sita said to her friend: 'Look at the sky this afternoon, it is like a white-washed wall. Once upon a time I lived in a house with white walls. Every year during Diwali, my father white-washed our walls with lime and powdered sand.'

'Where is your father?' asked Rukmani. Sita shrugged her shoulders. 'He is dead. All are dead. Cholera got them all four years ago. There were five deaths in my family. My father, my mother, my three brothers ...'

'But what happened to that house with the white walls?' asked Rukmani.

'That must have died too,' said Sita laughing.

'Everything dies, Rukmani. Even the sky.' Rukmani looked up at the blanched brilliance of the sky. It hurt her eyes.

Ayee called the young girls to her side in the afternoon. 'Come, let me do your hair for you,' she said. First, it was Rukmani's turn. Ayee removed the snarls from her curly hair and plaited it tight. Rukmani wrinkled her face in discomfort. 'I shall get you Brahmani oil for your hair,' said Ayee. 'Then in two months time, it will have more body. Your hair is too soft and silky. Sita's is thick enough. In fact, she is too weak to carry the burden of her hair.'

While their hair was being done, Sindhuthai climbed up the steps beside the porch, rubbing gratingly her rough feet on the stone. She cleared her throat and said: 'How are you today, my younger sister, you look happy today.'

Ayee grew pale at the thought of the hag's evil eye. 'We are pulling on, thanks to the blessings of Lord Ganesh,' said Ayee. 'Sita here is not too well. She has lost her appetite for food.'

'Has she attained puberty?' asked Sindhuthai.

'No,' said Ayee. 'Otherwise, I would not have been so thoroughly upset. I am wondering if I should take her to the doctor saheb today.'

'Don't you take your girls to the doctor saheb every week?' asked Sindhuthai. It was another of her loaded questions.

Ayee squirmed in embarrassment. 'Why do you ask such a question?' she asked the old woman. 'Has that bitch Koushalya been telling you that I do not get my girls medically checked up every week?'

'Yes, that was what she told me yesterday,' said Sindhuthai. 'I was passing by her house on my way to the ration shop when she stopped me. She insisted on my going in, to take a glass of tea with her. How could I refuse the offer and incur her displeasure? You know well what a lot of mischief she is capable of when her ire is aroused. Koushalya will make a deadly foe for anyone who irritates her. She has of late become very influential too. I saw the car of a high government official parked near her place.'

'How does she manage it,' asked Ayee, 'with her scummy bunch of girls?'

'They are well-trained,' said the hag.

'I am taking my girls this very minute to the doctor saheb's dispensary,' said Ayee. 'I am sorry I cannot sit here talking to you, Sindhuthai.'

'I understand, sister,' said the hag, picking up shreds of

tobacco from the box. 'I am feeling weak and dizzy today,' said Sindhuthai. 'Younger sister, have you any money you can spare for a soda? Soda settles my stomach each time I feel ill.'

'Sindhuthai, you don't mean soda, do you?' asked Ayee. 'You drink country liquor whenever you can lay your hands on it. The Inspector Saheb himself told me that he saw you buy a bottle of moosambi.'

'Scandalmongers all over the place,' cried out the hag. 'Everybody hates me nowadays. In my time, I have helped all of you in many ways. Now nobody loves me. All make fun of me. When youth goes away every woman becomes an object of ridicule. Lachmi, you have a house now, but watch my words, after another ten years you will be thrown out from here like a rind and another will become the Ayee of this place. Most probably Mira. Or that dark one Saraswati.'

'Don't say such things with your accursed tongue, Sindhuthai,' cried out Ayee. 'My girls will always love me. I have never ill-treated them. Ask Rukmani here. Ask them all how I have fed them, and how I have nursed them with my own hands during illness. They will not throw me out as your girls once threw you out, Sindhuthai. I will be their Ayee until my death.'

Sindhuthai chortled sarcastically: 'This is what I too thought once upon a time, Lachmi,' she said, 'but see what happened. My favourite girls threw me out calling me names. What could I do? I was past the age for attracting any man. All I could do was roam around looking for a hut to live in, a shelter over my head. I begged at street corners for a year. Then I became a useful member of this locality. I could perform abortions for as little as twenty rupees. So you invited me into your houses. I was lucky. But how can you be sure that you will be as lucky as I have been?'

Ayee hid her round dark face in the folds of her sari and

wept unashamedly. Sita remembered the gurgling sound the buffaloes made while they wallowed in the muddy pools of her village. How funny Ayee's sobs sounded. She nudged Rukmani with an elbow. She wanted suddenly to giggle. But Rukmani was watching the fat woman cry, intently and with a sympathetic expression on her face.

Mira called out from inside: 'Rukmani, come here for a minute. I cannot hook my choli which is open at the back.'

Rukmani went inside to help Mira who was standing dressed only in a satin petticoat of black and an open choli. She looked radiantly happy. She had a red spot of sindoor on her brow and kajal in her eyes: 'Mirathai, are you going out anywhere?' asked the little girl.

'Oh, no, I am dressing to meet my friend who is coming this evening,' said Mira.

'You look like a married woman,' said the girl and Mira embraced her with a sudden laugh.

'I am married,' said Mira, 'but don't tell anybody about it ...'

'Are you married to the student who visits you,' asked Rukmani, 'the one who sold his fountain pen to come to you?'

'Yes, he is my husband. He is called Krishna. Is that not strange, Rukmani?' Mira asked the little girl. 'Is it not strange that I am Mira and he is Krishna?'

Rukmani remained silent. She felt Mirathai was behaving peculiarly that evening. It was like the delirium of those who have high fever. There was a red flush on her high cheek bones and a glitter in her eyes. Mira decorated her hair with a string of mogra flowers and bit her lips to make them redder. 'Why don't you use some lipstick?' asked Rukmani.

'He does not like lipstick,' said Mira.

When Rukmani had finished hooking her choli, Mira hugged her with passion and kissed her forehead. 'God bless you, my child,' said Mira.

When she went out in the porch, Ayee had stopped her crying and Sindhuthai had vanished. Rukmani sat on the steps near Sita who was watching the buses go by. 'One day, Ayee took us in a double-decker bus,' said Sita. 'Then I put out my hand and plucked a guava from a tree.'

'You are a liar,' said Rukmani.

'Ask Ayee,' whispered Sita. 'I plucked a ripe guava from the tree. I ate it on the bus. It was full of seeds. I liked the seeds the best of all. Ayee said that the guava seeds produce worms in the stomach. Long wriggly worms.'

'Maybe you have such worms in your stomach,' said Rukmani. 'That is why you threw up last night ...'

'I threw up because I cannot any longer stand being messed up by men. I hate all of them.'

'Don't you want to get married?' asked Rukmani. 'Don't you want a home of your own and a few children?'

'Yes, I would love to have a home of my own and a few children. I want a plump baby to dandle on my knee. I want him to smile at me and call me Ma. But I don't want to have any man in my house.'

A client entered hiding his face from the passers-by. 'You are very early,' said Ayee, 'it is not yet evening.'

'I am busy in the evening,' said the man. He wore a white bushshirt and terylene trousers which looked dirty. He looked around him nervously and bit his nails.

'All right, make your choice,' said Ayee gesturing towards the group of girls. Except Mira, all were seated on the porch. Radha was as usual showing a lot of her things sitting in a careless posture. The man signalled to her and she rose obediently to escort him indoors.

From Mira's room rose the lilting tune of Jayadeva's *Gitagovinda*. 'Mira sings beautifully,' said Ayee.

The girls listened in silence.

Ratisukha sare gathamabhi sare madana manohara
vesham.
Nakuru nithabini gamanavilambhana manusarathum
hridayesham Radhe!

*

It was only towards the morning that Ayee discovered that Mira had eloped with the college student. Mira's room was shut and the other girls knocked on the door casually while passing, calling out: 'Mirathai, did he leave you so exhausted that you cannot even get up from your bed?' There was no angry answer, no light laughter. 'Come and eat your breakfast,' cried Radha, knocking hard at the door. Breakfast was served at six every morning, a heavy meal of parathas dripping with vanaspati and an egg curry. There was a glass of milk to top the meal. After partaking of this meal the girls normally curled up on their mats and fell asleep until it was time again for the next meal which was at two. It was only after five that they stirred themselves to attend to their toilet. The bath was elaborate and afterwards their hair was decked with strings of flowers, and rouge was rubbed into the skin of their cheeks to make them look healthy. Beneath the pink powder the bare skin was ashen and seemed to have aged prematurely. Using their bodies as rinds had killed their spirits. Only the young children, Rukmani and Sita, laughed normally. But they hardly knew the significance of the sexual act. For them, it came as an occasional punishment meted out for some obscure reason. Perhaps the mistake they committed was that they got born as girls in a society that regarded the female as a burden, a liability. The two girls resented the frequent interruptions during their game of squares and even while the coarse men, old enough to be their grandfathers, took the pleasure off their young bodies, the children's minds were far away, hopping in the large squares of the chalked diagram on the floor of the porch.

When Radha pushed open the door, she found Mira's room empty except for the bed that was not slept in. Her tin-trunk, containing the coloured saris she was fond of wearing, had disappeared. On the window sill lay a cracked mirror, as small as Mira's palm, and some sindoor, spilt on the edge. 'Where has our Mirathai gone?' asked Radha clutching at her own brow. 'Has she run away with that crazy student of hers?' Ayee sat on Mira's bed and wept with a great deal of emotion. 'My golden bird has flown out of her cage' she wailed while from outside the window a crow cawed rapidly as though it had also heard the shocking news. And was perturbed. Radha smoothed Ayee's hair and spoke soothing words. 'She is sure to return,' she said. 'That fellow has no money with him. After they have sold Mirathai's gold chain and have lived off its price they will come back to beg for food.' Still Ayee continued with her wailing which rose higher, higher, until the neighbours rushed in to seek the cause of her grief. Koushalya was the first to arrive. 'What has happened, elder sister?' she asked Ayee.

'My Mira has been kidnapped by my enemies,' said Ayee. 'All were jealous of her beauty. All the high government officials came asking for her. And rich businessmen. Now I am lost. There is no girl here who can lure in men the way my Mira could. What a golden skin she had. What a body. I shall go to Benaras this week and die there.'

'Mira must have gone willingly,' said Koushalya. 'Such things have happened before, and in the best of houses. Didn't that Nepali girl fly the coop last year from Marine Drive? Let her go and perish. You must not upset yourself about an ungrateful girl.'

'You know how I looked after the girls here, Koushalya?' asked Ayee. 'I used to give them parathas made in ghee, eggs, milk, and cod-liver-oil tablets. I used to take them to all the melas and the exhibitions going on in the city. I loved them deeply …'

'Elder sister, you are too kind,' said Koushalya. 'I have been wanting to warn you about being overkind to these girls. Kindness does not beget kindness. I whip them whenever they make a mistake and so they fear me. My girls are docile. They will not play hopscotch on the porch all through the afternoon like your young ones. You know that it is illegal to subject minors to a life of prostitution, don't you? People are beginning to talk about your house. People who are your so-called friends. I shall not mention their names.'

'Who talked about my girls?' asked Ayee, rising from Mira's bed, with red eyes. 'Was it that witch Sindhuthai? Was it the Inspector Saheb?'

Koushalya shook her head enigmatically and smiled. 'I did not come here to gossip,' she said. 'I wanted only to comfort you.'

Ayee embraced Koushalya with a new-found affection. 'You are kind to me,' she said. 'We should stick together,' said Koushalya. 'We have common enemies. If we are united none can harm us, not even the police …'

The dark girl Saraswati immediately moved her things into Mira's room. 'I get more clients than anyone else,' she said in explanation. 'I have always had an eye on this room. This looks out on the wide street. I can sit at the window-sill and charm the men who go about in motor cars.'

Radha sulked. But she could not afford to argue with Saraswati who brought in an income higher than hers. 'She is common,' she murmured in another's ear, 'have you seen how she swings her fleshy hips, this way, that way, when any man is looking at her? …'

Ayee kept whining about the ingratitude of Mira, seated on the charpoy in the porch while the labourers and the mill-hands walked past nonchalantly. When the Inspector came in, it was past noon, and he asked her incredulously, 'Lachmibai, why did you not inform me earlier?' Ayee beat a slow tattoo on her dark forehead and continued wailing monotonously. 'If I had known of this earlier, I would have brought back the erring wench by now,' the Inspector said. 'I would have had my men to comb the railway platform and the bus stops and would have by now sent that rogue to our jail. Now they must be far away from the city, probably in some village trying to find work.'

'What is the use trying to jail the boy?' asked Ayee. 'Mira went willingly. She is not a minor either. Rukmani told me that Mira had secretly married the boy.'

'Marriage,' shouted the Inspector. 'Why would a decent boy marry a prostitute? He will set up practice as a pimp and earn money from her. Lachmibai, you are much too innocent to guess the ways of this shrewd world. That hussy refused to let me touch her; do you know that? One day, I offered her thirty rupees and yet she said "No Inspector Saheb, I cannot be unfaithful to the man I love." Is that the way a girl from a decent brothel like yours talks to an influential man like me? I could have thrashed her then and there with my cane but I did not want to create a ruckus in your house. You are like my elder sister, Lachmibai.'

'You speak the truth, Inspector Saheb,' cried Ayee. 'You are my brother. In times of distress, I look to you for guidance. Without your help, I would not have flourished in this locality. I often wonder why I cannot take my girls and move to a better locality, Grant Road or Colaba for instance. My girls have class, don't they? My little moppet Rukmani has charmed every client who has come here. She has such a supple body, such a clean smell. Inspector Saheb, she was telling me yesterday that she liked you immensely. She called you a handsome man.'

'Where is the girl?' asked the man, trying to peer into the darkness of the corridor. 'She must be lying asleep in the hall,' said Ayee. 'She wept the most when Mira disappeared. Mira used to bathe her in the mornings and sing songs to her.'

'May I see Rukmani for a few minutes?' asked the man.

Ayee went inside to call the little girl and found her playing with two plastic dolls, dressing them up to look like a wedded pair. Sita lay on the floor, sideways, watching her.

'The Inspector Saheb wishes to see you child,' whispered Ayee to Rukmani. 'Leave your dolls and go to the little room next to mine. I shall send him there ...'

'Ayee, not now,' protested the child. 'We are playing a game just now. We are about to marry our doll off to the new doll bought yesterday. We have named them Mira and Krishna. Please ask that horrid man to go away.'

Ayee bent down and tweaked her ear. 'Get up this very minute,' she said. 'You cannot afford to displease the Inspector Saheb. He is a very important man. If he wants you now you must go and please him. I do not want disobedience from you.'

'All right, Ayee,' said the girl, rising slowly from the floor. 'Wait for me, Sita, I shall be back in a short while to complete the wedding ceremony.' Sita smiled wanly, still lying on the floor.

The Inspector Saheb was very gentle with the young girl. 'Do you want me to buy you a doll that opens and closes its eyes?' he asked her, fondling her chubby arms. 'Yes,' said Rukmani. 'There is such a doll in a shop at Churchgate,' said the man. 'It cries "Mummy" when you press it on its stomach. It is a foreign doll. It costs about hundred rupees. But I do not mind spending the money on you if you are kind to me off and on. I love you more than I love anyone else in this world.'

'What about your wife and children?' asked the child.

'I do not love them the way I love you, Rukmani,' he said. 'I have a granddaughter of your age, but even her I cannot love the way I love you. I will get you toys every month if you promise to remain kind to me. I am not good looking like that student who carried Mira away but I have a soft heart inside me. I am ugly. I am like a monkey, am I not? Do you feel an urge to laugh at me when you see my face?'

Rukmani felt moved by the man's humility. 'You are not ugly,' she said. 'You are a little bit like my father who left us and went away. Whenever I see you I remember him.'

'You will never be unhappy again in your life, my darling,' cried the Inspector. 'I shall protect you. I shall ask Lachmibai to keep you away from all clients except myself. You can be my keep. I shall pay her a fixed sum of money so that she will not complain. Will you like that arrangement?'

'But what will happen when some young man comes forward and asks me to marry him?' asked the girl.

'I shall be that young man, my mogra flower,' whispered the man hoarsely, holding her tight.

Rukmani felt a slight nausea when she was assailed by the mouldy smell of his scalp where white hair grew in untidy patches. But she closed her eyes immediately and lay passive, thinking of the foreign doll that cost hundred rupees.

*

When Rukmani saw Sindhuthai go into the little room next to Ayee's with a lump of green paste, resembling ground mehndi leaves and a sharp stick, she had a sense of foreboding. Sita had already been taken to the room, Ayee dragging her by her thin arms, while the child cried out, 'No, no Ayee, I do not want that hag to touch me.' The door was locked from within but Rukmani stood near the door trying to listen to the sounds from inside. She could hear Sindhuthai's shrill voice chiding Sita and then the girl's slow whimper. Later, there was a shriek which was muffled midway by somebody's rough hands. Rukmani felt her legs weaken. What were they doing to her friend, Sita?

Rukmani walked over to the bars of the porch and looked out. A double-decker bus rumbled along the road carrying in it men who stared at her. The sky was once again like a newly whitewashed wall. She remembered what Sita had told her of the little house in the village where five deaths took place in a month. Then at that precise moment she heard the scream which did not sound like a human voice at all. Was it some kind of a beast that had escaped from the zoo, she wondered. After a few minutes, Sindhuthai came out and quietly sat herself down on Ayee's charpoy. She picked up a drying leaf from the betel box and began to chew. 'Our Sita is in a grave condition,' she said. 'I think she may even die.'

Rukmani ran into the house. The door of the small room was half open. Ayee and Radha were tucking old saris between Sita's thighs. Blood was soaking through the clothes rapidly. Sita lay insensate like a doll. How pale she looked with the rash of the midday sun mottling her narrow face. She resembled a foreign doll. Only her belly seemed alive, protruding from her flat body like a growth. Would she utter 'Mummy' when she was pressed on her tummy, like that expensive doll? 'Rukmani, our Sita is going away,' sighed Ayee, speaking in a soft voice. 'She is going to paradise where all the good people go after death.' 'Is Sita dying?' asked Rukmani. None answered.

The Inspector was very helpful during the next few hours. He brought the Doctor to write down the medical report, and after another hour, the body was taken to the electric crematorium and burnt down to ash in the presence of Ayee and three of the older girls. What remained of Sita was only a plastic doll bought from a street hawker, a light green male doll which was named Krishna by Rukmani and was married to the other doll. Rukmani lay between the two dolls in the evening, shedding tears in silence. When a client knocked at the door, Radha whispered to him: 'Please go away today, we have had a tragedy at the house this morning,' and he left without much protest.

That night Rukmani woke up to hear a male voice coming from Saraswati's room. Saraswati's period of mourning did not last long. Rukmani felt all of a sudden a need for emotional security. If only Ayee put an arm around her shoulders and comforted her, she would sleep well again. She felt the presence of Sita in the room. If only the Inspector Saheb could come and take her to the little room and tell her that he loved her more than all …

The next morning, Ayee called an astrologer to the house. He drew a diagram on the floor and spread out some cowries in each of the squares. 'You are certainly passing through an unfavourable dasa in your life,' he said. 'You said that a girl eloped from here with a client and that another girl died. More calamities will follow, if you do not do a puja to control the evil stars who are your enemies.'

'Stars are my enemies?' asked Ayee. 'Even stars have turned against me. I have several enemies in this locality. All are jealous of me. I shall not of course mention names. I was planning to move to a better place, Marine Drive or Pasta Lane in Colaba. Would that give me peace of mind?'

'Getting a new place will cost you a fortune. The pugree itself will be a lakh,' said the astrologer. 'This place is well located. All you need to do is a havan which will cost you only a thousand at the most. All your foes will be wiped out. Your business will thrive.'

'Can you find someone to do it for me?' asked Ayee.

The astrologer glanced with lewd eyes at the girls lounging around on the porch. 'I shall myself perform it,' he said. 'But it has to be done in secret. Is there a back veranda in this house?'

After the astrologer left, Sindhuthai arrived to comfort Ayee. 'It is God's will, younger sister,' she said. 'Otherwise why would such a young girl become pregnant? She had not even attained her puberty. Such a thing is unheard of. Sita was not destined to live long. She had all the signs of one who is to die early in life. Don't you remember her pale lips? Her frail wrists?'

Ayee began to weep. 'She was such an affectionate girl,' said Ayee. 'She used to prepare my paan for me in the afternoons. A village procurer sold her to me for three hundred rupees when she was only ten. Her parents had died of cholera. I gave her cod-liver oil every winter but she did not put on any weight. Then one day, the Inspector Saheb told me that I should stop trying to make her fat. "She has the lithe body of a dancer," he told me. "Teach her to dance. She will charm your rich clients." I was planning to send her to a school to teach her some Bharatanatyam. But God has taken away my sweet child. Sindhuthai, please don't tell anyone what really happened. The doctor saheb wrote in the certificate that her appendix burst.'

'What is this appendix you are talking about? Is it the womb?' asked the old hag. 'No, no, it is something else,' said Ayee.

'Be more careful in the future, Lachmi,' said Sindhuthai, 'don't take chances. Rukmani should not be left to her fate. She too can become pregnant. She is well-developed.' 'Ah, Rukmani, she is not going to be in trouble,' said Ayee. 'The Inspector Saheb has taken a great fancy to her. She is to be his keep. He is too old to have children. He must be quite old.'

'No man is too old to procreate, Lachmibai,' said Sindhuthai. 'I have known of a case when an eighty-year-old man married a twenty-year-old girl and gave her two sons. The Inspector Saheb is a lion among men. He is virile enough to populate one whole planet.'

Ayee laughed and together with her laugh rose the dissonant cackle of the old hag.

'Do you want bangles?' asked a bangle seller who stopped at their front door. He held strapped to his shoulders a heavy case of wood and glass which contained bangles of myriad hues. Rukmani rushed forward to look at them. He sat down on the floor and took out a few cardboard rolls.

Each such roll bore on it about three dozens of plastic bangles. 'May I have a look at the orange ones?' asked Saraswati, thrusting forward her dimpled arm. 'Are they nylon ones?' she asked the bangle seller. 'Yes they are expensive,' he said. 'Do you think I cannot afford your nylon bangles, my good man?' asked the dark girl with mocking eyes. The man gave her a knowing smile. 'You can afford even gold ones, lady,' he whispered. She laughed, and her laugh was like the tinkle of silver bells.

'Don't you want to buy some bangles for yourself, Rukmani?' asked Ayee. 'The red ones of nylon will look good on your arms.'

Rukmani shook her head. The bangles suddenly reminded her of Sita and then the desire to wear them on her own wrists went away. 'No, Ayee, I do not want any,' she said.

Saraswati coaxed the man to put around her wrists, squeezing her palms, a dozen of the orange-coloured bangles. 'What if I don't pay you?' she asked coquettishly. The man grinned sheepishly.

'You do not have to pay me,' he said. 'What kind of a businessman are you?' asked Saraswati taunting him. He smiled at her, noting for the first time her full breasts straining at the thin red voile of her choli and her wide haunches. 'I am not much of a businessman,' he retorted, 'but I am a man all right. Do you want me to prove it to you?' Saraswati laughed aloud. She went inside the house to bring out the money. 'Where are you from?' asked Ayee. 'I am from Benaras,' said the man. 'My brother has a paan-shop near Dadar and we stay together at Koliwada.' 'Are you making a lot of money selling paan?' asked Ayee. 'No, Mother. We are just pulling on...' Just then the

Inspector Saheb entered the house. He was perspiring profusely. 'Everything is taken care of,' he said. 'I want now to lie down and relax for an hour. Where is Rukmani? Ah here she is ...'

Ayee thrust the little girl into the room with the Inspector Saheb. Rukmani leaned against the shut door and stared at the fat man on the bed. He had already taken off most of his clothes. His baton lay near the pillow. 'Come to me, my moppet,' he pleaded, his voice thickening with lust. Rukmani did not move.

'Are you angry with me, darling?' asked the man. 'Are you angry because I did not get you the foreign doll from Churchgate today? You know how busy I was today with that girl's death and her cremation and all the technicalities connected with the events? Give me time. In three days' time the doll will be yours. You can call her Sita in honour of your playmate ...'

Then Rukmani for the first time after her friend's death, broke down. She rushed towards the man and hid her sobbing face in the bushy growth of hair on his deep chest. 'Papa, papa,' she called out, sobbing, while the man, stupefied beyond words, kept stroking her curly hair. 'Oh papa, take me away from here,' she said, 'otherwise I too will die ...'

The man kissed her forehead. Lust had suddenly retreated. 'Papa. Is that what you called your father?' he asked.

'Yes,' said Rukmani. 'Papa was very fond of me. But he quarrelled with my mother, and left our home without even telling me that he was going away. He did not ever return. Before Diwali, I used to wait for him near our house, hoping that he would bring me a new frock, but he did not come. He will never come to see me again, will he? He has forgotten me, hasn't he?'

'Don't cry, my child,' said the Inspector, 'You have me as your papa. I shall from now on treat you like my daughter. Is that enough, Rukmani?'

Rukmani lay cradled in his arms and fell asleep. She dreamt that Sita and she were travelling by a double-decker bus and that they were plucking ripe guavas from tall trees and eating them, seeds and all ...

*

When Mirathai returned, her clothes dishevelled and herself very hysterical, Ayee was taking a short nap in the afternoon, open-mouthed like a crocodile lying in wait for the dragonflies that might settle on its tongue. She looked hideous in sleep. Rukmani was seated on the floor watching Ayee asleep.

Mirathai fell on the ample bosom of the old woman and began to weep. 'Help me Ayee,' she cried, 'the Inspector Saheb has ordered his constables to thrash him to death. They are torturing him at the police chowki. At this rate, he will fall down dead in an hour's time and I shall be a widow. Please go and tell them to stop beating him.' Ayee stared at the young woman. No emotion showed on her dark face. 'What has happened, Mira?' she asked slowly. 'You have decided to return ...'

'They are thrashing him to death,' cried Mira. 'Get up, Ayee, and tell the Inspector Saheb that he is not at fault. I was not kidnapped from here. I coaxed him to take me away. Then why should he bear the punishment while I am let off free?' 'Where is this boy, Mira?' asked Ayee.

'He is at the police station,' said Mirathai. 'Please let him go free. I shall remain here for the rest of my life.'

Ayee got up from her charpoy and ate a paan. 'All right, I shall go there and speak to the Inspector Saheb. You go inside and take a bath. Ask Radha to give you a good meal. You look as if you have been starving for a week.' Mirathai kissed Ayee's hands in gratitude and went into the interior of the house. So our Mira has come back, said Ayee to herself. She walked towards the police station, escorted by Rukmani. 'Falling in love with men is a dangerous thing,' she told the little girl. 'It is like tying oneself with a rope. If you do not love any man you remain free. Please remember that.'

The young man had been beaten black and blue by the time Ayee reached the police station to plead with the Inspector, for mercy. But soon, she was carrying him back to her house in a tonga, triumphantly, while he sat with his face bent and tears streaming from his eyes. 'It is not my fault,' he mumbled once. But Ayee did not bother to converse with him.

When the tonga stopped near their house, Ayee asked the young man to alight. He was helped down by Rukmani. 'All my bones are broken,' said the boy.

'There is a letter for you today, mother of the house,' exclaimed the postman stopping his cycle. 'Open it and read it out to me, Rukmani,' cried Ayee. 'Can it be that my son has finally forgiven his sinner of a mother?'

The groaning young man limped into the house and sat down. The postman was lingering on to hear the contents of the long-awaited missive. Rukmani read: 'Dear Ayee, I have remained silent for ten years but today my master who is a learned man showed me what true love means. He scolded me for having hurt you and for having abandoned you for years. He said that every profession has its own code of honour and that I ought not to have felt ashamed of you. He is a rich man owning a motor garage but he says that he will gladly give all his possessions if he were to be given back his mother who has been dead for ten years. You can earn money, you can get wives and children, but a mother lost is a mother lost forever, he said. Therefore, at his persuasion, I am writing to inform you that I shall be coming over to visit you this Saturday in the afternoon. Your loving son, Sadashiv Mane.'

Ayee burst into tears. Rukmani felt tears filling her own eyes. Even the postman was turning emotional. 'This is happy news,' he said. Ayee took out of her waistband a rupee note and handed it to the postman. 'See, how wise he has become, my son, my little son Sadashiv,' said Ayee blowing her nose violently. Just then, Mira came out and saw the young man seated, still as a statue, on the floor. 'Forgive me,' she said, falling on the floor and clutching at his feet. 'If I had not forced you to take me away from here nobody would have beaten you. Are you hurt badly? May I bring you some warm milk? Come and lie down for an hour.'

'Mira, let him be,' said Ayee. 'Give him some peace. He has suffered all this because of you. Now leave him alone to find his own peace.'

'What peace can he find without me?' asked Mira. 'Is he not in love with me?'

The boy stretched himself on the floor and closed his eyes.

'Don't you love me still?' asked Mira.

'I don't know,' said the boy.

'You go home to your mother now,' said Ayee. 'She must be so upset about your absence from home.'

'She could not have been upset,' said the young man, 'because both she and my father were away visiting a relative at Poona. Today she is expected back at seven in the evening. I shall get home before she comes ...'

'Was this to be merely a week's holiday, a short idyll?' asked Mira, a sob rising in her throat. 'Were you lying to me when you said that we were going to live as husband and wife?'

The boy was silent.

'How old are you, son?' asked Ayee, chewing betel leaves. 'I am nineteen,' said the boy. 'Go home to your mother and forget all about Mira,' said Ayee. 'Come to us after you get yourself a job and can afford to visit prostitutes.'

Mira flinched at the words. The boy rose, and folding his hands in a salute, he walked away.

'The ungrateful swine,' hissed Mira. 'He told me that he

was twenty-four and that he had found a job at a mill. A liar. A stinking liar.'

Mira threw out Saraswati's things from her former room. There was a lot of trouble then. Saraswati scratched Mira's fair face. 'You slut,' she called out to Mira, 'you think you own this place? You run wild with a schoolboy for a week and return home as though nothing has happened. I shall not let you have this room. It belongs rightfully to me.'

It was a question of seniority. Ayee could not take Mira's side this time. Mira had erred. Of that, there was no doubt at all. Saraswati was the most qualified of the lot, the one who was totally devoid of emotion and was the most professional of all. She deserved the best room.

Mira gave in and took a corner of the common hall where the juniors slept. She had to start rehabilitating herself again.

When the Inspector Saheb came, Ayee brought forth for him a plate of laddus. He smiled at her. 'What are you celebrating today?' he asked her. Then the letter was once again read out and once again tears flowed copiously from several pairs of eyes. 'Your luck is changing, Lachmibai,' he said. Then he called Rukmani gesturing with his hand and held out the large parcel which was with him. 'Open it and see what I have brought for you, my daughter,' he said.

Of course, it was the foreign doll. It did resemble Sita to some extent. Its vinyl-skin was very pale and its tummy had a bulge. Rukmani pressed it and made it squeak out the word Mummy. Rukmani kissed the doll all over its face and on its half-opened hands. 'No kiss for your papa?' asked the Inspector. She embraced him with her free hand and rubbed her nose on his shirt-front. 'You are getting very sentimental,' said Ayee to the Inspector. He nodded and gave another of his wide smiles. 'Lachmibai, I am an old man now,' he said. 'This child reminds me of my granddaughter who is staying with her parents at

Nagpur. She is sweet and affectionate like this one. Sends me a sweet letter every year at Diwali time.'

'There is nothing like affection, Inspector Saheb,' said Ayee. She kneaded the tobacco shreds with lime in the hollow of her left palm. 'I am also not as young as I used to be. I wonder why I cannot leave this house in Saraswati's hands and go to Benaras to die. I have enough money saved up to live in comfort until the last day of my life. Perhaps I shall carry some with me, an old woman for company, perhaps our Sindhuthai. She has no relatives. I shall make up my mind after seeing my son this Saturday.'

'We will miss you, Lachmibai,' said the Inspector. 'This house will not be the same without you. And, Rukmani. Where will she go? She will have to be at the mercy of the new Ayee of the house …'

'I shall marry her off to my son,' said Ayee. 'Surely, he can now support a wife.'

'Am I too early?' Asked a client walking in, furtively glancing around. 'You can never be too early in this house,' said Saraswati coming forward to lead him into the room inside. He eyed her with appreciation.

'Would you like to spend some time with our Mira?' asked Ayee to the Inspector. 'You have always liked her.'

'No, Lachmi bai, I do not feel like playing with a woman today,' said the man, applying lime on the leaves of the betel carefully. 'Something has died in me today.'

'Perhaps something has been born inside you today,' said Ayee with a tender grin. Rukmani's doll kept crying out Mummy, Mummy, Mummy …

Notes on Contributors

Shanichari

MAHASWETA DEVI was born in 1926 in Dhaka and educated in Shantiniketan. After finishing her master's in English literature from Calcutta University, Devi began working as a teacher and journalist. Her first book, *Jhansir Rani*, was published in 1956. Since then she has published twenty collections of short stories and close to a hundred novels, primarily in Bengali. Her important literary works include *Aranyer Adhikar, Hazar Churasir Ma, Chetti Munda O Tar Tir*. She has also been a regular contributor to many literary magazines such as *Bortika*, a journal dedicated to the cause of oppressed communities in India. One of the most eminent writers of modern India, she is the recipient of many prestigious awards such as the Jnanpith, Sahitya Akademi and Magsaysay awards, as well as the Padma Shri from the Government of India. Her works have been translated into many languages.

SARMISTHA DUTTA GUPTA is a journalist and a freelance editor.

Rebati

PHAKIRMOHAN SENAPATHY (1843–1918) was the father of the modern Oriya short story. 'Lachhamania', the first short story he wrote remains untraced, hence 'Rebati', also written by him, is considered to be the first short story written in Oriya. His autobiography, *Atma-Jivana-Carita,* is an authentic record of the contemporary socio-economic-political conditions of Orissa that prevailed during his time. Dr J.V. Boulton, a renowned professor in the School of Oriental and African Studies, London University, UK, translated his autobiography entitled *My Times and I* into English, which has been published by the Orissa Sahitya Akademi. A versatile genius, Phakirmohan was dubbed by the readers of Orissa as 'Vyasakavi' for his vast literary creations.

ADYASHA DAS has been writing poetry in English as well as her mother-tongue, Oriya, since her school days. She has two books of poems to her credit, *Nemesis* and *Anucharita*, the latter a collection of Oriya poems. She has also taken up several projects in translation. A post-graduate from Delhi School of Economics and subsequently an MBA with specialization in Human Resource Management/ Organizational Behaviour, she now teaches at the Indian Institute of Tourism and Travel Management, Ministry of Tourism, Government of India.

Girls

MRINAL PANDE published her first short story in the Hindi weekly *Dharmyug* in 1967 and, since then, has expanded her repertoire from the short story to the novel and then to musical drama. Her first collection of short stories, *Darmiyan* (1977) won an Uttar Pradesh State award, while *Shabdavedi* (1980) was judged the best work produced by a young author. As a professional journalist, she writes on Hindi literature, art, film, and on women's issues. She has been the editor of *Vama* and *Saptahik Hindustan*, executive editor of *Hindustan Dainik*, and senior editorial adviser to NDTV. She is currently the group editor of the Hindi publications of the Hindustan Times house: the daily *Hindustan*, a monthly digest, *Kadambini*, and a magazine for children, *Nandan*. She is the founder president of the Indian Women's Press Corps, and was appointed to the government's

National Commission on Self-Employed Women. Her published works in English include *Daughter's Daughter*, *Devi: Tales of the Goddess in our Time*, *My Own Witness* and *Stepping Out: Life and Sexuality in Rural India*.

RAMA BARU has done her master's in Social Work and is a doctorate in Public Health. Her published works include *Privatization of Health Care in India: Social Characteristics and Trends,* published by Sage Publications in 1998. She currently holds the post of Associate Professor at the Centre for Medicine and Community Health, Jawaharlal Nehru University, New Delhi.

Izzat

ASHAPURNA DEVI was born in 1909 into a traditional and conservative Bengali family. Since her family did not believe in formal education for girls, she taught herself to read and write. A prolific writer of short stories and novels, she wrote primarily at night after all her household chores were over. At just thirteen years of age she published *Sishushathi* in which the poem 'Ghare Bairer Daak' and the story 'Pashapashi' won critical acclaim. Her literary career spanned almost five decades. Her most popular novels were *Prathom Pratishruti*, *Subarnalata* and *Bakulkatha*. She won the Jnanpith Award in 1976.

RIMLI BHATTACHARYA is a comparatist by training. She taught English at Jawaharlal Nehru University for many years and is presently on a fellowship from the Indian Council for Social Sciences Research.

Kanjak

AMRITA PRITAM was born in Gujranwala, now in Pakistan, in 1919. In 1947 Amrita moved to Delhi and began writing in

Hindi. Today she is best known as a poet in her mother tongue, Punjabi, and as a prose writer in Hindi. Her writings after 1960 deal more and more with women who acknowledge their desires and their independence. Among her explicitly feminist fiction are her novels *Erial* and *Ik Sit Anita*. She won the Jnanpith Award in 1973 for her novel *Kagaz te Kanvas* and was awarded the Padma Shri by the Government of India in 1969. In the sensational *Aksharon ki Chaya Mein* (1977) she acknowledges the autobiographical core in each of her stories that deal with husband-wife relationships and the loneliness of married women. Four of Amrita's books—*Black Rose, The Skeleton and Other Stories, Existence* and *Revenue Stamp*—as well as several poems have been published in English translations.

HARBANS SINGH (1921–1998) was one of the most distinguished scholars of Sikh history and literature in the twentieth century. He started his career as a professor of English literature at Khalsa College and retired as the Chair of the department of religious studies at the Punjabi University, Patiala. He was a prolific writer throughout his life. His books include *Aspects of Punjabi Literature, The Heritage of the Sikhs, Guru Nanak and Origins of the Sikh Faith, Maharaja Ranjit Singh, Bhai Vir Singh, Guru Gobind Singh* (which was translated into fourteen Indian languages), *Guru Tegh Bahadur* and *The Berkeley Lectures on Sikhism*. He also contributed numerous articles to leading journals and newspapers, and loved translating Punjabi authors into English. His final accomplishment is the monumental four-volume *Encyclopaedia of Sikhism*.

Death Comes Cheap

BABURAO RAMCHANDRA BAGUL was born in 1930 in Nashik, Maharashtra. Educated in Nashik, he later went to the Dadar Vidya Mandir, Mumbai, from where he did his MSc. He edited a magazine, *Amhi*, but it soon closed down. He then wrote for a number of magazines. His first collection of short stories, *Jenvha Me Jaat Chorli Hoti*, was soon followed by another called *Maran Swasta Hot Ahe* in 1969 for which he received the Maharashtra State award. His popular novels include *Sood*, *Sardar*, *Bhoomiheen*, *Pavashya*, *Mooknayak* and *Pashan*. He was appointed member of the Maharashtra State Textbook Research Committee for Marathi textbooks. He has written a number of thought-provoking articles on Dalit literature and on the problems faced by Dalits in India.

SANDHYA PANDEY was born in Amravati, Maharashtra. She did her BSc. in Microbiology from Bombay University and MA in English literature from Nagpur University. She taught English in junior college in Amravati and in Mumbai for a brief while and then worked with *Mid-Day*, Mumbai, as a reporter. She has translated Kishor Shantabai Kale's *Kolhatyache Por* into English.

The Swing

J. BHAGYALAKSHMI has published short stories, poems, features, articles, interviews and literary criticism in leading magazines and newspapers in English and Telugu. Her published works include *Ivy Compton-Burnett and Her Art*, *Capital Witness: G.K. Reddy* (ed.), a collection of poems titled *Happiness Unbound*, two volumes of Telugu short stories and a number of translated works. She is trained in mass communication and has taught at the Indian Institute of Mass Communication. At present she is a columnist, freelance journalist and media consultant.

My Mother, Her Crime

AMBAI (C.S. LAKSHMI) was born into a large family in 1944. She wrote several stories for *Kanaiyazhi* in the early seventies. Around that time she was also part of the Chennai-based group that published the journal *Pregnyai*. *Siragugal Muriyum*, her first collection of short stories, was published in 1976, and the second collection, *Veettin Muulaiyil Oru Samayalarai*, was published in 1988. In 1984 she published a critical work in English, *The Face Behind the Mask*, a study of the images of women in modern Tamil fiction by women writers. She also writes scripts for her husband, Vishnu Mathur's films. She has recently worked on an illustrated social history of women in Tamil Nadu and has established SPARROW, Sound and Picture Archives for Research on Women.

LAKSHMI HOLMSTRÖM is a freelance writer and translator who studied at Chennai and Oxford. She is the author of *Indian Fiction in English: The Novels of R.K. Narayan* (1971) and editor of *The Inner Courtyard: Short Stories by Indian Women* (1990) and *Figures in a Landscape* (1994), a collection of stories from India for young readers. She has translated novels and short stories by contemporary Tamil writers, including Ashokamitran's *Water* (1993) and *Neermai*, a collection of short stories by Na Muthuswamy (1995). Her retelling of two ancient Tamil narrative poems, *Silappadikaram* and *Manimekalai*, was published by Orient Longman in 1996.

Mushi

PRATIBHA RAY was born in 1943 in Cuttack, Orissa. Pratibha Ray's first novel, *Barasha Basanta Baisakha*, was published in 1974. She has won the Orissa Sahitya Akademi Award (1985) for her novel *Shilapadma*, and the Moorti Devi Award from

Bharatiya Jnanpith (1985) for her novel *Yagnaseni*, which tells the story of Draupadi through a series of letters. She has also won the Katha Prize for the best story in 1991, and was felicitated by Bharatiya Jnanpith on their Golden Jubilee celebration for her contribution to Indian literature in 1995. Her well-known novels include *Punyatoya* (1979), *Nilatrushna* (1981), *Shilapadma* (1983), *Yagnaseni* (1985), *Uttaramarga* (1988), *Mahamoha* (1997). She has also written a number of short stories and primers for children. Pratibha Ray lives with her husband and her three children in Bhubaneswar. She is currently a Reader in the Education Department in Ravenshaw College, Cuttack.

BIKRAM K. DAS, formerly Professor of English at CIEFL, Hyderabad, and the National University of Singapore, received the Sahitya Akademi Translation Award in 1989 for his translation of Gopinath Mohanty's *Paraja*. His translation of Pratibha Ray's *Adibhoomi* was runner-up for the Crossword Prize, 2001. He has done several other translations of Oriya fiction and poetry. He now lives in Bhubaneswar.

I See the Yamuna on the Horizon

INDIRA GOSWAMI (b. 1942) started writing when she was fifteen. She is the author of about 700 short stories, twenty-five novels, including *Dontal Hatir Une Khowda Howda*, *Nilakanthi Braja* and *Tej aru Dhulire Dhusarita Prshtha*, and many other books, such as *Ramayana from Ganga to Brahamputra*. She is the recipient of a number of prestigious awards: the Sahitya Akademi Award for her novel *Mamare Dhara Tarwal* (1983), the Assam Sahitya Sabha Award (1988), the Bharat Nirman Award (1989), the Sauhardya Award (1992), the Katha Award (1993) and the Jnanpith Award (2001). She was also awarded the International Tulsi Award on the occasion of the

International Conference on Tulsi Das held in Florida International University in 1999 for her work on the Assamese and Hindi Ramayanas. Her autobiography, *Adhalekha Dastaveja*, and its English translation were published in 1988, and have won critical acclaim in India. She is currently Professor in the Department of Modern Indian Languages and Literary Studies, Delhi University.

ATREYI GOHAIN has a master's degree in English literature. Currently she is an editor with a reputed publishing house. She translates stories from Assamese to English.

A Memory Called Ammacchi

VAIDEHI is the pseudonym of Janaki Srinivasa Murthy who lives in Manipal, Karnataka. She was born in 1945. Vaidehi has to her credit a novel, *Asprushyaru*, poems, a collection of short stories, the recorded memoirs of K.L. Karanth, several translations including that of Kamaladevi Chattopadhyay's *Indian Women's Struggle for Freedom,* children's plays and a collection of essays. Her stories and poems are prescribed texts in the Universities of Mangalore and Mysore. She has received several awards including the Geetha Desai Datti Nidhi Award (1985, 1992), the Katha Award for Creative Fiction (1992), the Karnataka Sahitya Akademi Award (1993) and the M.K. Indira Award (1994).

PRANAVA MANJARI N. has taught in a postgraduate women's college in Bangalore for five years. Her Ph.D thesis focusses on Russian literature. She lives in Delhi and devotes herself to special interests like translation and book reviews.

The Quilt

ISMAT CHUGHTAI (1911–1991) was born in Badayun, a small town in Uttar Pradesh, and spent her early years in Jodhpur where her father was a civil servant. Despite her elite background and the freedom she had managed to win for herself at home, she had to fight for her education. After a brief stint as a teacher at a girls' school in Bareilly, Ismat went on to Aligarh Muslim University to train as a teacher. However, she and six other women had to lobby for admission and were allowed to register only if they would sit in purdah. In this period she started writing secretly, and succeeded in carving a niche for herself among her contemporary Urdu fiction writers—Rajinder Singh Bedi, Saadat Hasan Manto and Krishan Chander. In 1941 she married Shahid Latif, a filmmaker, with whom she had two daughters. Ismat played an active role in the Progressive Writers' Movement in the thirties and forties, but spoke vehemently against its orthodoxy and inflexibility.

M. ASADUDDIN translates Assamese, Bengali, Urdu, Hindi and English. He writes on the art of translation and fiction in Indian languages. He has recently edited *For Freedom's Sake: Stories and Sketches of Saadat Hasan Manto* (Karachi: Oxford University Press, 2001) and edited with Mushirul Hasan *Image and Representation: Studies of Muslim Lives in India* (Delhi: Oxford University Press, 2000). A former fellow at the British Centre for Literary Translation, University of East Anglia, UK, he currently teaches English literature and Translation Studies at Jamia Millia Islamia, New Delhi.

A Doll for Rukmani

KAMALA DAS was born in 1934. She publishes her work in Malayalam under the pseudonym Madhavikutty. She was married when she was fifteen, to her uncle K. Madhava Das and, except for brief stints in Calcutta and Delhi, the couple has lived in Bombay. In December 1999, Kamala Das converted to Islam and changed her name to Suraiya. Her first collection of short stories, *Mathilukal*, was published in 1955. *Pathu Kathakal* followed in 1958 and *Narichirukal Parakkumpol* in 1960. Some of her works in English include the novel *Alphabet of Lust* (1977), a collection of short stories called *Padmavati the Harlot and Other Stories* (1992), in addition to five books of poetry, *Summer in Calcutta* (1965), *The Descendants* (1967), *The Old Playhouse and Other Poems* (1973), *The Anamalai Poems* (1985) and *Only the Soul Knows How to Sing* (1996). Some of her more recent novels in Malayalam are *Palayan* (1990), *Neypayasam* (1991) and *Dayarikkurippukal* (1992). Her autobiography, *My Story*, has been translated into fifteen languages.

Copyright Acknowledgements

The editor and the publishers gratefully acknowledge the following for permission to reprint copyright material:

Seagull Books, Calcutta, for 'Shanichari' by Mahasweta Devi, first published in 2002 by Seagull Books, Calcutta, in an English translation by Sarmistha Dutta Gupta in *Outcast: Four Stories*;

Mrinal Pande and Rama Baru for 'Girls' by Mrinal Pande;

Katha, New Delhi, and Garutman, for 'Izzat' by Ashapurna Devi, first published in the collection *Separate Journeys*, published by Katha and Garutman in 1998; the copyright for the English translation rests with Garutman, an organization that aspires to publish quality Indian literature;

Amrita Pritam and Nikki Guninder Singh for 'Kanjak' by Amrita Pritam;

Baburao Bagul for 'Death Comes Cheap' by Baburao Bagul;

J. Bhagyalakshmi for 'The Swing' by J. Bhagyalakshmi, originally published in Telugu in *Bhumika* (March–April 2002);

East West Books (Madras) Pvt. Ltd and the author for 'My Mother, Her Crime' by C.S. Lakshmi, published by East West Books (Madras) Pvt. Ltd, in an English translation by Lakshmi Holmström, in *A Purple Sea*;

Pratibha Ray and Bikram Das for 'Mushi' by Pratibha Ray;

Indira Goswami and Atreyi Gohain for 'I See the Yamuna on the Horizon' by Indira Goswami;

Katha, New Delhi, for 'A Memory Called Ammachi' by Vaidehi, first published in Kannada as 'Ammacchiyemba Nenapu' in *Udayavani*, November 1996, Manipal. The story won the Katha award for fiction in 1997. This translation appeared in *Katha Prize Stories 7* and won the Katha Award for Translation in 1997. The copyright for the English translation rests with Katha, a registered, non-profit society devoted to enhancing the pleasures of reading;

Penguin Books India, New Delhi, and M. Asaduddin for 'The Quilt' by Ismat Chughtai;

Kamala Das for 'A Doll for Rukmani'.